MELVIN /

ZOMBIE HUNTER

For Nan.

A CIP catalogue record for this title is available from the British Library.

ISBN 978-0-9932000-7-6

Illustrated by Marek Jugucki
marek@mjcartoons.co.uk
www.mjcartoons.co.uk
Twitter: @mjcartoons

Designed by Amy Doorbar

Published by Creative Educational Press Ltd,
2, The Walled Garden, Grange Park Drive, Biddulph, Staffs, ST8 7TA
www.thecepress.com
www.alanpeat.com
Twitter: @alanpeat
Facebook: Alan Peat Ltd

Printed by York Publishing Services Ltd,
64, Hallfield Road, Layerthorpe, York, YO31 7ZQ
www.yps-publishing.co.uk

About the author

Mathew Sullivan was born and raised in Stockport. As a young lad, he was obsessed with comics and Lego. Now, as a grown man, he is obsessed with... comics and Lego. And drinking tea.

He is currently learning to play the guitar, and is a demon on a pair of rollerblades.

However, he can't cook for toffee, and his handwriting is pretty atrocious.

In his spare time, Mathew enjoys exercising and going to the gym in a vain attempt to be as strong as the superheroes whom he so admires. No-one has yet mistaken him for the Man of Steel.

Mathew currently lives in Manchester. He has no pets, but he does have a vast, truly precious collection of action figures.

MelViN McGee: ZoMbie HuNter

Part 1: THe OutbreaK

Chapter 1: Meet Melvin

Here are a few things that your average ten-year-old boy worries about:

- Their friends finding out that their bedtime is really eight o'clock, when they've told everyone that they're allowed to stay up till eleven.
- Playing computer games too loudly and waking up their best mate's angry dad, who works nights.
- Ripping a hole in their brand new school trousers after their mum **SPECIFICALLY TOLD THEM THAT IF IT HAPPENED AGAIN THEY'D BE SENT BACK TO SCHOOL IN THEIR OLD, ITCHY SHORTS!**

Here are a few things that ten-year-old Melvin McGee worries about:

- Running low on grabble-goo-tipped bolts for his crossbow.
- The fact that there's only one tub of his favourite *Flobby Jenkins Chocotastic Spread* left on the shelf of the abandoned, armoured supermarket where he lives.
- The smell of rotting meat coming from the overturned delivery truck outside, which could well attract the attention of a few of the more inquisitive grabbles.

You see, our friend Melvin McGee is a grabble hunter...and "grabble" is a slightly nicer alternative to the word...

ZOMbie.

Now, before we find out how a ten-year-old boy managed to get himself the prestigious (yet fairly hazardous) job of 'Head Grabble Hunter of the Town of Flinchester', let me clear up a few zombie misconceptions:

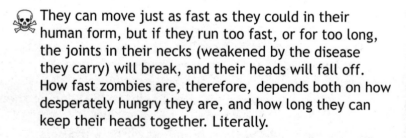 They can move just as fast as they could in their human form, but if they run too fast, or for too long, the joints in their necks (weakened by the disease they carry) will break, and their heads will fall off. How fast zombies are, therefore, depends both on how desperately hungry they are, and how long they can keep their heads together. Literally.

Zombies are quite particular about **how** they eat. Just as some people suck the chocolate from Twix bars before eating the biscuit, many zombies deal with human fingers and toes in a similar way. It's the same with Crème Eggs and eyeballs, for that matter.

💀 Zombies won't attack you if you smear shoe polish (or 'grabble-goo') on yourself. Chronic zombie indigestion (aka 'grabble gut'), caused by trying to eat toes through tough leather shoes, has led to a serious aversion to the smell. That said, this nasal camouflage won't work if you are cut or bleeding. Zombies can smell a drop of blood from 100 metres, and no amount of shoe polish will put them off *that* delicious aroma.

💀 The contagious grabble disease is carried in their green saliva, so their bite is their most dangerous weapon. However, in moments of severe hunger, zombies have been known to use body parts as projectiles. It is not unheard of for a grabble to pull its own arm off, simply to have something to throw at a potential victim.

💀 A zombie's vocabulary is severely limited. They tend to communicate via grunts, the range of which is limited to four meanings:
- I'm hungry
- Over there/here
- Mine
- One day I'm going to be on X Factor

The last one might seem

odd, but it's a leftover habit from years of reality TV overload.

Finally, **zombies are <u>not</u> dead.** They are just very, very poorly. Unfortunately, this particular strain of illness turns them into mindless, ravenous, brain-munching monsters, and there's not much anyone has been able to do about it so far...

So, how does our mate Melvin fit into all this?

Well, it all started on the day of his tenth birthday.

Chapter 2: Happty Burpday

That morning, Melvin had been woken early by the sound of a large flock of squawking birds streaking over the roof of his house. Bleary-eyed and fuzzy-headed, he dragged himself from his pillow and looked out of the window just in time to see the tail-end of the feathered foghorns. They were headed away at speed, leaving in their wake a whole street's worth of howling dogs and hissing cats. Had Melvin known why all these animals were so agitated, he might well have dived back into bed and hidden under the covers, permanently. But this rude awakening was swiftly forgotten as the realisation that it was his **birthday** dawned upon him. Leaping from his bed, Melvin scrambled across the landing, banging like a jackhammer on the other bedroom doors as he went.

"**Mum! Dad! Wake up!** Jessica, rise and shine-a-light! It's only my flipping **birthday** isn't it?"

Having pinballed his way through the house, Melvin reached the bathroom. Grabbing his toothbrush (the blue one with the vibrating bristles that tickled his teeth) and the toothpaste (also blue, but with no tickle factor to speak of) he looked at himself in the mirror.

Melvin was pretty tall for his age. He was what some people describe as 'lanky', 'a beanpole', or 'all arms and legs'. **He** preferred the terms 'athletic', 'lean', 'wiry', or at the very least, 'svelte'. He had short, messy blond hair, which he worked extremely hard to keep looking stylishly messy all day, using a concoction of waxes, putties and pastes. He had steely grey eyes, a slightly upturned nose, and a smile that was quirkily crooked. When Melvin smiled, it looked like only half of his face had realised something was funny. However, truth be told, Melvin was a kind-hearted boy who spent most of his days with that crooked smile permanently plastered on his face. And today being his birthday, Melvin's half-smile almost threatened to take over the lazy side of his face too.

One quick wash and rinse later, Melvin was back in his room, throwing on his school uniform whilst still reminding anyone in shouting distance that it was, in fact, his birthday, and that they really should get out of bed, right now. In fact not now, now was too late. Five minutes ago. Yes indeed, the party started five minutes ago. Uniform on, Melvin flung himself down the stairs, shouting like a demented town crier as he went,

     "Come on you lazy lot! You've got until the toaster pops to get yourself downstairs! *Don't make me come back up there!"*

As Melvin careered around the corner and burst into the kitchen, he was met by an almighty scream...

"SURPRISE!"

If it had been physically possible to do so (and not considerably bad for his health) Melvin would have leaped clean out of his skin. The shock quickly subsided though, as Melvin saw his mum, dad and little sister gathered around the table, still in their pyjamas, with the fetching addition of multi-coloured paper party hats. A huge banner hung from the handle of the freezer door, all the way across the kitchen, to the cupboards on the other side. It read,

Happty Burpday Melbin!

Melvin instantly recognised it as the handiwork of his four-year-old sister, Jessica. She stood on a chair, clapping her hands and beaming with pride at her work, equally happy to see 'Melbin's' crooked smile creeping (almost) across his whole face. Her blonde, scruffy hair and light eyes matched his, but her smile was so wide and toothy that when she grinned you could be forgiven for thinking her head was in serious danger of coming unhinged and falling off. Although she couldn't have been out of bed for more than fifteen minutes, this scruffy little creature had already managed to get toothpaste in her eyebrows and milk in her slippers. Nonetheless, Melvin ran to her, lifted her from her chair and gave her a great big, brotherly hug.

"Happty Burpday Melbin!" Jessica announced as she squeezed Melvin's neck, slightly tighter than was comfortable.

"Easy there Jessibobs! You'll wring the young, innocent life out of me; I've only just made it to ten years old!" Melvin said as he placed Jessica back onto the chair carefully and smiled up at his mum and dad.

Melvin's mum was called Jane, and she was the kindest, most thoughtful person Melvin knew. She was one of those rare people who put everyone else before themselves, without even really thinking about it. She was always there to hug Melvin when he was hurt, cheer him when he did well, console him when he was upset, help him when he was stuck, and most importantly, provide him with sparkling clean, floral-smelling, neatly ironed underpants, every single day of the year, including Christmas. In other words, she was a top mum. Even now, stood there in her crinkled nightie, with her half-flattened, half-stuck up bed-hair, she was still every bit the beautiful, warm and kind-hearted woman that Melvin was proud to call his mum.

Melvin's dad, Martin, on the other hand, had managed to comb his hair and brush his teeth (without getting so much as a **speck** of toothpaste in his eyebrows) and looked every bit as polished and organised as he always did. Melvin quickly put two and two together. This was all his dad's doing. **He** was the one who had got up earlier than anyone, washed and dressed in ninja-stealthy silence, made his way downstairs, hung the banner, and even sorted the slices of toast with the '10' written in jam. Melvin's dad had thought of **everything**, like he always did, and by now Melvin's smile was so wide that, for a moment, you might have mistaken him for his own smiley, scruffy sister. After a large and lingering family hug, the whole McGee clan sat down to eat a delicious (although not really very nutritious) birthday breakfast, featuring cereal bowls filled with equal parts of Choco-Flakes and ice cream. As was his usual morning habit, Martin McGee picked up the daily newspaper. He opened it and flapped the pages a few times, revealing a rather disturbing headline to the rest of the table:

DEADLY DISEASE DRIVES DOCTORS DOOLALLY

MYSTERY OUTBREAK CAUSING MADNESS IN MILTINGTON

Chapter 3: The Caretaker's Warning

One flurrying whirlwind of lunch box packing, P.E. kit finding, toothpaste removing and coat putter-on-er-ing later, Jane, Jessica and Melvin McGee clambered into the car and set off to school, while Martin left for his job as manager of the local SuperSave store. As they drove through the town of Flinchester, passing the arcade, the cinema, the pub and the swimming pool, Melvin stared out of the window in deep contemplation. What would life be like now that he was ten, he wondered? He was, after all, all grown up now. Best start thinking about grown up stuff, like facial hair, chinos and button-down collars, sensible shoes (with good arch support), prudent pension schemes, and of course, the colour **beige**. Even as they passed by the town zoo, which usually drew a crooked smile from Melvin, he remained lost in thoughts of practical family vehicles and dinner parties.

Melvin was so distracted, he didn't even hear the slightly panicked news broadcaster on the radio saying something about 'the first case of a deadly virus'. Words like 'deranged', 'ravenous', 'biting' and 'infection' whistled through one ear and out of the other as Melvin battled with his future choice of carpeted versus polished-wood flooring. However, the moment Jane McGee pulled into the car park of Green Oaks Primary School, and he spotted his best friends with another giant banner, this one reading 'Happy Birthday, you old fogey!', Melvin realised that being ten was going to be just as much fun as being nine.

After plenty of high-fives, slapped-backs, and the occasional knuckle-rub to his already scruffy-haired noggin,

Melvin and his friends made their way to class. As they shoved boisterously through the door, they were greeted by a disturbing sight; their headteacher, Mrs Graves, sitting in the teacher's chair, eyeing them coldly through her grey, steel-rimmed spectacles. Mrs Graves had a perpetually sour look on her face. She looked the way a cat might look if you tried to give it a cold bath – extremely displeased; immensely irritated; and poised to hiss and spit at a moment's notice.

"McGEE!" she screeched in a shrill, ear-piercing tone. "Is a simple BIRTHDAY any excuse to come bouldering into this classroom like an ELEPHANT with BALANCE ISSUES?"

"No Mrs Graaaaaaaves," Melvin responded in his standard, doleful, 'talking-to-the-teacher' voice.

"Being ten is NOTHING to get excited about, believe you me. It's just one more step towards BALDNESS, WEIGHT-GAIN and PAYING TAXES. Now SIT DOWN, the lot of you."

Melvin and his pals trudged to their seats. They were the last ones in, and as they got settled, Mrs Graves rose, closed the classroom door, and turned to address the class.

"As the more astute among you may have noticed, I am NOT your teacher. Mr Woods is off sick; a sudden and violent case of food poisoning, apparently. You will therefore have a SUPPLY TEACHER for the day."

Supply.

Teacher.

The words **every** school child longs to hear, perhaps even more than, "Today we are watching a video," or the ever popular, "The school has been closed due to heavy snow." The moment those two glorious, wonderful words escaped from Mrs Graves's shrivelled, miserable lips, Melvin and his friends knew exactly what they were going to do.

Cue an entire morning of swapping names, sitting where they liked, making up insane "Class Rules" ("Yeah, Mr Woods always lets us stick pencils up our noses, Miss!") and even throwing a few fake accents in to boot. Melvin fully indulged in the wonder of the supply teacher. This one was a poor, timid lady, who looked so old she might well have been wheeled out of the local nursing home to take the class. Melvin's name for the day was 'Scotty Parkinson', which was actually his best friend's name. Scotty had, in turn, adopted the name 'Laurence Jacobs', and so on.

By the time the lunch bell sounded, both sides of Melvin's face hurt from the effort of trapping laughter in his mouth all morning. As his gang re-formed and headed out to the playground, the laughter finally exploded, like a firework filled with giggles. As they started planning tricks for the afternoon, the gang's merriment was so loud that Melvin only just picked out a very odd noise, coming from behind the caretaker's office. It was sort of a mix of muttering, screaming, stomping and smashing. He shushed the group so that they could hear it, then they all crept round to investigate.

"I **TOLD** zem...vouldn't listen."

BANG. CRASH. THRASH.

"Knew it...flipping idiots...do zey know what zey've DONE?"

BOOM. WALLOP. THUD.

"Doomed uz all...zis iz zee **END**!"

"...Errrrr...Mr Plant? Are you alright, sir?"

In that moment, Melvin seemed to be the only one capable of speech. The sight of the usually quiet, calm and friendly school caretaker, Mr Plant, now kicking holes in storage boxes, tearing a newspaper into confetti, and speaking in an odd accent had left the rambunctious group utterly silent.

In a situation like this – when a person's private tantrum has been interrupted – the ranting individual usually freezes, like a hare in headlights, then straightens themselves up and offers some daft excuse before scuttling away in embarrassment. Not so Mr Plant. He marched woodenly up to Melvin, ribbons of torn paper clenched tightly in his hands, shook his fists under Melvin's chin, then paused, cleared his throat and growled,

"Do I **LOOK** alright, Melvin? **No**, I am not alright! In fact, if 'alright' was hydrogen on the periodic table, I'd be somewhere around **RADON** right now!"

Melvin stared at Mr Plant with a look of utter confusion, partly because he didn't know what the periodic table was, and partly because he did not recognise this character as the same man who had spent the last six months fixing leaks and moving bins around the school. Mr Plant obviously

sensed the confusion.

"Don't they teach you **ANYTHING** these days? No surprise really, I'll bet it was some young hot-shot, know-nothing sniveller who ignored all my warnings and caused all **THIS**." Mr Plant shook the remnants of the newspaper in Melvin's face while he spoke. Melvin still had absolutely no idea what he was on about. Maybe too much school mince for dinner had driven him round the bend.

"**GO** Melvin. Go. All of you. Get as far away from Flinchester as you can. Find somewhere safe... and hide. Whatever you do, stay away from **THEM**."

Melvin could see that this was no mince-induced madness. Mr Plant was genuinely furious... and genuinely terrified. But terrified of **what**?

"Who are **THEY** Mr Plant? What are you talking about?"

Mr Plant opened his mouth as if to elucidate. But his speech was cut short by a bloodcurdling sound from the other side of the playground...

It was the sound of a little girl's scream.

Chapter 4: Mr Woods Returns...Kind Of

That sound. That awful sound. That blood-curdling, bone-chilling cry of pure terror. It reverberated through the concrete of the playground like a shockwave, immobilising everyone in its path. Melvin scanned the crowd of fear-frozen statues and spotted a sudden blur of movement. He quickly realised that it was the girl who was responsible for the terrifying wail, and she was moving at break-neck pace. Quite how this was possible, he wasn't sure; this tiny mite looked like she would have all the lung power of a wheezy mouse, and the athletic ability to match. And yet, she was bolting through the crowd as fast as her little legs could possibly go, heading back towards the school.

Melvin turned to see what, exactly, was propelling the child at such extreme volume and velocity across the school yard. At the end of the playground he saw a strange, lumbering shape. It was big; bigger than anything else on the yard, and it was moving awkwardly; shuffling and limping. Squinting, Melvin realised that it was a man, a man dressed in stained, torn clothes, the holes in which exposed pallid, grey skin. Melvin could only just hear a disturbing moaning sound coming from the mysterious figure. As confused as he was shocked, Melvin managed to take a few tentative steps forward. He instantly wished he hadn't, as that small journey brought with it the distressing realisation that this ghoulish looking *thing* was, in fact, his **teacher**, Mr Woods.

Only it wasn't the Mr Woods that Melvin knew. His usually bright eyes were sunken and yellow, and his mouth hung open like a dustbin lid, dripping green saliva on to the

yard. His fingers, bent and crooked, had curled into claws, and his whole body was twisted into the most unnatural shape. This was **not** food poisoning. Mr Woods was not just 'off sick'. Something was very, very wrong...

The frozen children surrounding Melvin must have noticed the perturbed look on his face, because they all turned as one to look across the playground. After spotting the horrifying sight of 'Mr Woods', it didn't take long for the first statue to break free and run away screaming. This was the fuse that sparked complete uproar: a chaotic explosion of screeching children. They stampeded, like panicked pachyderms, back towards the school.

"NO! Not here... zey can't already be here. It's too soon! It's not ready yet!"

Melvin caught the tail end of Mr Plant's distressed mumblings, and he quickly realised that somehow, the caretaker knew **exactly** what was going on. But Melvin also knew that this wasn't quite the time to sit down for a cup of tea and talk it over. Explanations would have to wait. For now, Melvin did what everyone else was doing: he joined the herd and ran for it.

Melvin's gang was already far ahead of him. They hadn't exactly left him behind, but having been caught up in what he was seeing and hearing, Melvin had taken a little while longer to start running for dear life than the others. Most of the children were already streaming through classroom doors; some diving under tables, others huddling inside stock cupboards, some even burying themselves amongst the coats and P.E. kits in the cloakrooms. Hiding spaces were filling up fast, and Melvin knew that even if he made

it inside, that was no guarantee of safety. It's not like Mr
Woods was a stranger after all; he'd know every single way
in and out of that school, every nook and cranny. There
must be somewhere better, Melvin thought, but *where*?
Just then, he heard a noise ring out above the din of the
petrified mob. It was a car horn, accompanied by a familiar
voice...

"MELBIN!"

Legs still pedalling, Melvin looked out to the road that ran
parallel with the playground. There, he spotted his mum's
car, teetering half-on and half-off the pavement, with his
sister's screaming head sticking out of the sunroof like
some bizarre car ornament. His mother was screaming too,
gesturing desperately for Melvin to come to her. Melvin
could see that his mum was well and truly spooked, which
he didn't quite understand; how could she already know
what was happening? Nevertheless, he broke away from the
pack and ran to the fence, leapt over it and dived into his
mum's waiting arms.

"**Melvin!** Oh my goodness, thank heavens you're safe!
I heard there was one on the loose – we need to get out of
here!"

"One what? D-di-did you see Mr Woo-W-Woods? What's
the m-matter with him? What's g-go-going on mum?"
Melvin's tongue tripped over words as questions tumbled
uncontrollably from his mouth.

"I'll explain later my darling," his mum replied in the
calmest tone she could manage. "For now, just get in the
car. Seat belt on, we need to get to the SuperSave."

"Mum, I m-may not know exactly what is g-g-going on, but I'm pretty sure this isn't the t-t-time to shop!"

Jane pushed Melvin into his seat, locked all the doors, started the car and gunned the engine. Melvin and Jessica were thrown back in their seats by the force of the acceleration. This must be serious, Melvin thought; if there were awards given for sensible, safe, painfully slow and tragically boring driving, his mum would win them all. To see her speeding and swerving through traffic, tyres skidding and horn honking all the way, was enough to turn Melvin and his sister white. They both grabbed the headrests in front of them and held on for dear life. Eventually, in a gap between skids and honks, Melvin just about managed to find some words and push them out of his terrified mouth,

"Please mum, tell me what's happening!"

Without taking her eyes of the road, Jane began to explain.

"Your dad rang. He saw an emergency news bulletin about a terrible disease which has broken out in three towns. It's spreading fast. The victims turn violent: they attack people."

The colour drained from Melvin's face as his mum continued her explanation.

"They've told everyone to get home and lock themselves indoors, but your dad managed to clear the store and activate the emergency security. There are heavy, steel shutters in front of all the windows and doors; he's turned the supermarket into a giant fortress. It's filled with supplies, and now all we have to do is make it there."

They'd have to hurry though, as by now the story was all over the news, and all around them, people were starting to panic...

Chapter 5: Darkness

SPLAT! Melvin was thrown sideways, his face suddenly flattened against the cold side window as his mother yanked the steering wheel all the way over to the right. The tortured tyres screamed and scrambled for grip, almost losing traction, yet somehow they carried the heavy vehicle around the final corner. Now it was a straight run to the SuperSave, where Martin McGee would be waiting.

"We're going to be OK kids; your dad is waiting for us. Everything is going to be..."

Jane McGee didn't see it coming, but Melvin did. That is one of the advantages, if you can call it an advantage, of having had your head thrown about in all directions. Melvin saw the other car, which had spun out of control; racing to safety no doubt, just like they were. It had skidded right into the curb, mounted the pavement, bounced through a wooden fence and across a garden, and had smashed straight into the side of the McGee escape wagon before Melvin had had the chance to say a thing. The impact had sent their car spinning, sliding and careering down the street, ricocheting off parked vehicles and sending pieces of torn bodywork and shattered glass flying into the air. Eventually, the car came to stop, just inches away from a rather large and unforgiving-looking tree. The McGee family sat, dazed and shaken, battered and bruised. Surprisingly, it was little Jessica McGee who spoke first,

"...DADDY!"

Jane and Melvin lifted their heads and looked down the road, where Jessica was pointing frantically. There, running towards them at full speed, was Martin McGee. As relieved as they were to see him, Melvin and his mum couldn't help but notice the terrified look on Martin's face. The look that told them that danger had not passed. The look that was actually focused not **on** them, but **behind** them. The look which forced Melvin and Jane to glance over their shoulders. Instantly, their faces turned grey, their eyes widened like saucers, and they began to scramble frantically at their seatbelts. For, out of the back window, they saw not one, not two, but at least **fifty** morbid, ghoulish, rotting creatures, all like Mr Woods, running, crawling, lurching and dragging themselves towards the crashed vehicle... towards them.

As Melvin's trembling fingers fumbled at the latch of his seatbelt, his mum opened the door opposite and pulled a now-screaming Jessica free. Melvin took a deep breath in an attempt to calm himself, focused hard on the latch, and finally heard the click that signalled his freedom. He let the seatbelt recoil and was reaching for the door handle, when WHAM! The first of the terrifying monsters threw themselves at the window. Its broken, ragged nails scratched the glass and it tore at the door frame – snarling and groaning – looking Melvin dead in the eye. For the second time that day, Melvin found himself frozen; paralysed with fear.

These creatures looked more horrifying the closer they got; this one had eyes that bulged, looking as if they might fall out of its head at any moment. Then, as if on cue, one of its eyes **did** fall out, swinging about on a long, red, stringy vein, like a pendulum on some gruesome grandfather clock. Melvin felt sick: this thing was repulsive. Its mouth hung open, black and rotting. Its limp green tongue lashed about like it had a mind of its own. Its skin hung, dripping off its bones, looking like it had been poured over its skeleton like candle wax. Worse than all these things, however, was the sight of a name badge hanging from the creature's torn clothes. A name badge that read 'Miranda'. Melvin recognised this as the lollipop lady from his school, the same lollipop lady who had helped him across the road countless times.

"Miranda?" Melvin began, but the monster didn't let up. With a final swing of its decaying arm, it finally broke through the window and grabbed hold of Melvin's jumper.

Melvin started to scream.

All of a sudden he felt an even stronger pull in the opposite direction. Had he been so distracted by Miranda that he had failed to notice another monster approaching from behind? He closed his eyes and waited for the worst, only to hear a familiar voice...

"Got you!"

It was Martin McGee, his strong arms pulling Melvin free from Monster Miranda's grasp and carrying him away. Before he knew it, Melvin was watching the pursuing army of mindless freaks from high on his dad's shoulder as Martin ran towards the SuperSave. Melvin heard his mother and sister shouting encouragement; they must be nearly there, he thought.

However, just as quickly as he had been lifted up, Melvin

was thrown violently from his father's shoulder and sent tumbling to the ground. He dragged himself up and turned to see his dad rolling around in a tussle with a ghastly creature which had sprung out at them from some nearby bushes. Melvin started towards the pair, intent on helping his dad. But just as Martin seemed to get the upper hand, two more revolting creatures appeared from the bushes and leapt into the fight. From the middle of the pile of bodies came a muffled, yet unmistakable voice,

"MELVIN... RUN!"

But Melvin **couldn't** run, he **couldn't** abandon his dad. He started to move forward once more, but yet again he felt a set of arms wrap around his waist, dragging him in the opposite direction. This time it was his mother, and although he protested, wriggled and tried to squirm free, she pulled him quickly to the main entrance of the SuperSave. The shutters were just high enough for them to crawl beneath. Jane McGee pushed her children inside and activated the closing mechanism, and Melvin could only watch as his father was buried under a mountain of grisly, hideous monstrosities.

The heavy, metal shutters finally slammed shut, and then there was only darkness.

Part 2: The Hunter

Chapter 6: Staying SuperSafe

There were a lot of tears that first night.

Melvin cried because of what he'd witnessed; his loving father torn away from him, taken by those awful, ravenous monsters. He felt helpless... he felt like a coward... a helpless coward who hadn't fought for his family like his brave dad had. He'd just let himself be bundled up and carried away. **Again**. These thoughts made Melvin cry harder and harder, although tears of sadness soon turned to tears of rage.

Jane cried too, but only in silence, and only in private. She knew that was what her children needed. If they saw their wonderful mum weeping like a leaky tap, they would be all the more upset. So, she fixed the best fake smile she could manage on her face, gathered Melvin and Jessica into her loving arms, and saved her tears until they were asleep.

Jessica also cried, mainly because she had missed her favourite TV show, *"Gooble and the Floobles"*. Though they never said it, Melvin and Jane felt glad that Jessica was upset about not seeing a bunch of weird purple aliens playing counting games and singing alphabet songs. Better that than her realising what was **really** going on.

***

The sun rose the next morning, sending slivers of sunlight slipping through the tiny cracks in the shutters of the SuperSave store. Soon the entire building was illuminated by a bizarre web of sunbeams, criss-crossing in all directions. The place was **enormous**. It wasn't your average small-town grocery shop, it was a megastore that sold an extensive variety of goods, organised into many different departments. The McGee family had somehow found their way in the darkness to the gardening department, and Jane had rested Melvin and Jessica against a large pile of garden turf, falling asleep with her children in her arms. As the sun moved, the enormous web of light changed shape around them, and one particularly bothersome ray fell straight across Melvin's face. It forced him to open one eye, and then the other. Both were still bloodshot, and stung from all the tears of the night before.

Melvin glanced across at his slumbering sister. To look at her, you would think nothing out of the ordinary had ever happened. Her hair looked like the usual atomic explosion of blonde frizz and dried jam, and her eyes darted about under her eyelids as she sucked her thumb and dreamed, no doubt of Gooble and his *"ABC, sing-with-me"* song. This made Melvin smile his crooked smile, and although it was only a small one, even by his standards, it was the first time he had smiled since school the day before.

As Melvin glanced upwards towards his mother, that crooked grin quickly retreated. He could see that she was dreaming too, but from the look on her face; the scrunched up, tearful eyes and the pained, gritted teeth, he could tell exactly what she was dreaming about. He hugged her tighter, and her face seemed to relax slightly. As he lay there, Melvin started to think about all that had happened in the last 24 hours. The monsters, the panic, Mr Plant's outburst, his dad, the reports on the radio...

The reports on the radio!

Maybe there would be some new information in the news today. Maybe someone had figured out exactly what the heck was going on... *someone* had to know *something*. Melvin decided to venture to the electronics department to see what he could find out.

Slipping out from his mother's protective embrace, Melvin stood and stretched his lanky limbs. Everything felt stiff and swollen; he had aches on top of aches. The floor of the SuperSave was not, as it turned out, a comfortable place to sleep. He rubbed his sore neck as he walked through the gardening department; rows of gleaming garden tools reflected sunlight into his tired eyes. Spades, rakes, trowels... and axes. Melvin couldn't help but wish his dad had grabbed one of these before venturing out to help them. He tried not to linger on this thought too much, as he felt the sting of tears in his tired eyes again, but instead pushed on through to the next shopping area, signposted '**Toys**'.

Now, every child will know what it is like to venture into the toy section of a big supermarket. It's pretty much as close as you can get to heaven on Earth. Or it would be, if you were ever **ALLOWED TO PLAY WITH ANYTHING**. But no, all the amazing toys; the action figure of your favourite cartoon hero which lights up in the dark AND shoots missiles from its rocket pack; the latest awesome computer game where you play as a ninja octopus which kills mutant squirrels; **THE bike**, you know the one, with suspension

front and back, TWENTY-ONE GEARS, and chrome stunt pegs; *everything* that would make life perfect, just sits there, on shelves, staring at you. And the moment you reach out for that one magical toy that will make your life complete, gazing at it with wide eyes and dribbling like an idiot, all you hear is...

"DON'T TOUCH THAT!"

Or...

"PUT THAT *DOWN!"*

Or maybe...

"THAT IS *NOT* A TOY!"

(Even though it quite clearly is, it's just not YOUR toy.)

"LOOK WITH YOUR **EYES,** NOT WITH YOUR **HANDS!"**

(Yeah, thanks for the sound advice, mum. I'm forever trying to see through my thumbs.)

"PUT IT ON YOUR **CHRISTMAS LIST!"**

(This classic only ever comes out between January and September, just in case you actually **do** put it on your Christmas list.)

But the thing is, no one was around to shout any of these

things at Melvin. As he stood in front of the most expensive, most shiny, most totally amazing-ist peddle buggy in the shop, he thought that it must be at least a two-minute walk over to the electronics department. Two *whole* minutes. **One hundred and twenty seconds.** That was ages! In the buggy, however, it would take him less than half a minute. Not to mention the fact that he was, after all, in a survival situation now: it was crucially important for him to conserve energy. The real question was: could he afford NOT to take the most awesome buggy in the shop and ride around in it?

Melvin quickly decided that, as his life so clearly depended on it, he should commandeer the buggy. In no time at all, Melvin was pedalling frantically down the central aisle of the SuperSave.

His new, totally necessary, life-saving buggy came equipped with a handbrake, and as the electronics department sped up to meet him, he pulled it hard and yanked the steering wheel all the way round. This sent him skidding to a stop, which would have looked mega-cool had anyone actually been around to see it. Clambering out of the buggy, Melvin noticed something very important. Even though there were no lights on in the SuperSave, there were tiny red lights flashing on all the electronic devices. This meant they still had **power**, at least for now. Melvin walked up to the biggest TV on display and switched it on.

He instantly wished he'd stayed cuddled up with his mum.

Chapter 7: The Grabbles

The news reporter, who stared out from the giant screen at Melvin, was a young, well-dressed, and even more well-spoken man. But, unlike the calm, composed, professional news reporters that Melvin was used to, this one was shaking and shivering like someone had turned his studio's air con to 'Arctic-Polar-Brass-Monkey-Sub-Zero-Freezer' setting. However, he couldn't possibly have been cold; he was sweating so profusely that patches of wetness had soaked through his shirt **and** his jacket. Furthermore, far from being clear and coherent in his speech, his words toppled clumsily out of his trembling mouth, and he stuttered terribly every time he attempted to say a particularly disturbing word like 'plague', 'contagion', or 'cannibal'.

There was one *other* word though, one extremely disconcerting and tremendously alarming word, which took the news reader a considerable amount of *extra* stammering, stuttering and sweating to get out...

ZOMbieS.

As if the reporter's garbled remarks weren't worrying enough, Melvin's eyes were drawn to the video feed in the top corner of the screen. It showed hordes of malformed monsters roaming through deserted streets. Some stopped to scratch and claw violently at the doors and windows of people's houses. Others dived hungrily into bins, or tried to smash their way into parked cars, using their own heads as battering rams. Even the way these freaks **moved** was disturbing. They looked like they hadn't been put together correctly, like each one of their twisted limbs wanted to scuttle off in its own direction. They were **truly** horrible.

Suddenly, Melvin's attention was drawn to the news reader once again as he fumbled over some more irksome words,

   "We must a-ad-advise viewers that the f-fo-following images are d-di-disturbing in nature..."

To save you from the same reaction as Melvin had (which was to throw up all over the gleaming floor of the SuperSave) let's just say that what the video showed included a close-up look at zombie eating habits. Let's also say that what the zombie was eating did, at one time, make up part of a **person**. The part which one would need in order to play football, wear trousers or generally just walk about. Melvin was so disgusted that he was about to switch the TV off, when the reporter started talking about where these monsters had **come from**. Considering that this was, after all, the point of Melvin's trip to electronics department; gaining a better idea of what was going on; he steadied his hand and continued to watch.

Here is what the reporter had to say (with nervous mumbles removed)...

ACTION NEWS - CHANNEL 10

"Here is your morning news, I'm Toby Jameson. In the past few hours more details have started to emerge regarding the zombie outbreak. It appears that the first sighting of the creatures was outside the grounds of a large food testing plant in the town of Miltington. The infection spread through the area within a couple of hours, as inhabitants were hit without warning. By 10:00 a.m., reports of infection were coming in from the neighbouring towns of Trablestock, Russelford, and Flinchester. At the end of Day One, reports of serious outbreaks had been received from almost every town in the county of Crodshire. As we move into Day Two of the epidemic, disease control procedures have been put in place in all surrounding counties, and those areas already affected are under full quarantine.

While scientists work hard to determine the cause of the disease, through their observations they have been able to offer some insights into the behaviour of the infected. The creatures seem to be weaker in the daytime, preferring shaded, secluded areas. Scientists are predicting that exposure to the summer sun, or other intense sources of heat, could cause them harm. Scientists have also witnessed a tendency amongst the creatures for rapid deterioration linked with excessive movement. In other words, if they move too quickly, they seem to fall apart.

There have also been reports from survivors who, although they have been scratched by

the zombies, have not been infected. It is therefore thought that the disease is transmitted through contact with saliva when a victim is bitten.

It has also been reported that a set of very particular items have been left behind in the aftermath of zombie attacks. On numerous sites, pairs of leather shoes and boots have been all that remain of human victims. While puzzled by this and other strange habits, scientists are working round the clock to find a solution to this terrifying epidemic. For now, authorities are advising people to stay inside, board up doors and windows, ration food and drink, and DO NOT approach the infected. We will be bringing you more news as events unfold."

Melvin listened intently, trying his best to ignore the harrowing images that still played on a loop in the top corner of the screen. He thought about what he had seen, and what he had heard...

"So, they don't like the heat, and they stay in the shade," he muttered to himself. "They can run, and climb, and crawl, but if they do any of that too much, or too fast, they fall apart. They can't infect you unless they bite you... and apparently... they don't like the taste of leather shoes?"

As a clearer image of the monsters formed in Melvin's mind, Mr Plant's rants suddenly came back to him,

I TOLD tHEM...WOULDn't LISTEn.

NO! NOt HERE...tHEy Can't aLREaDy BE HERE.

...IGnORED aLL MY WaRnInGS...CaUSED aLL THIS!

It's tOO SOOn! It's nOt REaDY yEt!

WHatEVER yOU DO, Stay aWay FROM THEM.

Mr Plant knew **something**... that much was clear. But the more Melvin let these ramblings ping around his brain, the more confused he became, and the more questions he had. **Who** did Mr Plant try to warn, and how did he know about the problem in the first place? What did he mean by 'they can't already be here'? Was he expecting them? And what about 'it's not ready'? What was 'it'? It sounded like Mr Plant was working on something, but what could a doddery old caretaker, who spent his days fixing leaky pipes and raking up leaves, be working on that would have anything to do with a zombie attack? Even the scientists on the news report seemed pretty clueless at this point. Melvin realised he needed to talk to Mr Plant, but that meant finding a way to cross a zombie-infested town and get all the way back to school. How could he possibly do that?

He couldn't... and he knew it.

Melvin slumped down against the TV display stand, lowered his head, and closed his eyes. The truth slowly dawned on him; they were stuck there... there was no way out.

Chapter 8: The Enemy at the Gate

An hour later, Melvin was still sitting on the floor of the SuperSave, lost in desperate thought, head drooping in defeat. Suddenly the hairs on the back of his exposed neck stood up. He felt hot breath, followed by the terrifying feeling of a slimy pair of hands wrapping tightly around his throat...

"**MELBIN!** Look, I got JAMMY FINGERS!"

Melvin, relieved from the initial shock, turned and saw his beaming little sister. He lifted her up; his mood instantly lightened, his problems temporarily forgotten.

"Jessy you mucky pup! How on earth did you get all jammy? Where is mum?"

"Mum is still sleepsies, she's being a dopey-Dora. Got jam from the jam bit! Why we in the shop Melbin?"

Melvin wasn't exactly sure how to answer that question, so he simply smiled and said, "Let's go and find mum."

Melvin set Jessica down and took her hand. They were about to head back to the gardening department, when Jessica caught sight of the TV beaming behind them.

"Melbin! TV! Want to watch Gooble and Floobles! A, B, D, sing and sneeze..."

Before Melvin could stop her, Jessica was off and running;

scampering back to the TV (which Melvin hadn't turned off). It was still on the news channel; the horrible images still beamed from the top corner; and now Jessica was stood in front of the giant screen, watching it all. Her bright eyes widened with fear, and her mouth dropped open.

She started to scream.

"MONSTERS MELBIN!" she sobbed, her words breaking between long wails and pitiful moans. "Why are there... monsters... on TV?"

Melvin ran up to the screen and turned it off, then he quickly knelt down and bundled his sister into his arms. He stroked her messy hair and gently shushed her crying. When she had calmed down enough, she spoke again. She was surprisingly composed, and tragically sure of her words,

"Daddy will make the monsters go away. Daddy always gets rid of the monsters in my room. Daddy is **brave**."

Melvin hugged his sister even tighter, mostly so that she couldn't see the tears that filled his eyes. Their dad *was* brave, but he'd already saved them once, and look what happened. This time it was Melvin's job... and he knew it.

"He is brave Jessy, and so are we. We are going to be just fine. Let's go and find mum."

The pair set off again, and as they walked, Melvin made up his mind. He **would** find his way back to school. He would find Mr Plant. He would do **whatever it took** to make his family safe.

After reuniting in the gardening section, which seemed to have become their new home, the family spent most of the morning gathering supplies from all over the SuperSave store. Jane took Jessica to get some food and drink, and Melvin was put in charge of improving their sleeping situation. Having found and assembled a tremendously luxurious family tent, Melvin furnished it with blow up mattresses, pillows, duvets, scatter cushions, and even some vanilla potpourri. He was determined to make things as comfortable and homely for his mum and sister as possible.

Plus, he just really liked the smell of vanilla potpourri.

On his way to find a nightlight for Jess, Melvin passed by the main entrance of the shop and noticed a mail hatch built into the heavy steel shutters. All day it had been quiet in the SuperSave, and there hadn't been so much as a peep from outside either. Melvin temporarily abandoned his supply mission and approached the hatch, intent on finding out just how Super**Safe** they really were in the Fortress of Groceries. He was about to lift the hatch when an awful thought struck him like a blow to the chest. The last thing he saw when looking out of those very shutters was his own father being buried under a pile of rotting, demonic fiends. What would he see now? His dad, transformed into one of those... **things**? Or worse, maybe just a pair of his dad's leather work shoes. Fear gripped Melvin; it seemed to trap his hand in mid-air. Try as he might, he couldn't reach any further towards the handle of the hatch...

"ENOUGH!" Melvin eventually said aloud, even though no-one was around to hear. "I'm sick to the back teeth of being **SCARED!**"

...and with that, Melvin thrust his hand forward, grabbed the handle and pulled the hatch open, forcing himself to look out into the street.

Carnage. It was sheer carnage out there. As he scanned the destruction, Melvin's eyes were drawn instinctively to the McGee family car: completely crumpled, savagely beaten, and sitting in a pile of shattered glass. Shockingly, it had actually come off quite well in comparison to what had happened in the rest of the street. Within his narrow, mail-hatch view alone, Melvin counted **five** overturned cars, two of which were blackened, twisted and melted after having been burnt out. Slightly further down the road, a once colourful, cheery ice cream van had suffered an even worse fate. It stood on its nose, pinned up against a tall tree. Bright packaging and dazzling sweets spilled out of the crushed serving hatch, like colourful intestines hanging out of a gaping, sugar-coated wound. There was, of course, no sign of any people. It appeared that all the survivors had taken the advice of the nervous news reporter and barricaded themselves in their homes. However, in the distance, through the shimmering haze of heat which rose from the trunk of an uprooted tree, Melvin saw something approaching.

There was no mystery this time, not like back in the playground. Melvin knew **exactly** what it was, and his chest instantly burned with furious anger. He forced himself to continue watching: he had to know what he was dealing with. As it got closer, Melvin could see that this particular zombie wore a shredded business suit, with a stained shirt and a tie that had been torn off just below the knot. It was also carrying something; an odd lump that flopped around as the creature stumbled forward. It rounded the fallen tree, passed the mutilated ice cream truck, and approached the McGee family car.

Then it stopped.

It sniffed the twisted metal.

It reached through the window and clawed at the seats.

Then, drawing its hand back, it raised the strange object it was carrying to its face. At that point, it took a very steady hand (and plenty of determination) for Melvin not to slam the hatch down and run back to his potpourri-scented den of duvets and pillows. For, as the monster chewed away on the object, Melvin recognised it as the same zombie snack from the video on the news story. He watched in disgust as the zombie tucked in like it was corn on the cob. However, just as it approached the ankle, the zombie launched its meal high into the sky and began to be violently sick. Now, a normal person being sick isn't the most pleasant thing to witness, but watching a decaying, slimy zombie chucking up its drastically foul guts was enough to put Melvin off his favourite *Flobby Jenkins Chocotastic Spread* for life.

"It's the shoes... again! They really can't stand them..." Melvin said, talking out loud. This time he wished he'd kept his thoughts to himself though, as no sooner had the words left his mouth, the creature's head snapped up sharply.

It glared straight at Melvin.

Melvin looked the creature right in its yellowed, veiny eyes as it started to run. He forced himself to maintain his position, watching the zombie's body contort and writhe

as it lolloped along. It had covered half the distance to the SuperSave, flailing wildly and howling like a scalded monkey, when one of its arms suddenly flew off. It sailed upwards, soaring through the air, and came to land in a tree. Melvin was astounded: the zombie didn't slow down; it didn't even flinch. It just kept coming, its remaining arm thrashing about, its twisted legs almost tripping over each other. As it neared the store it seemed to pick up more speed, and Melvin's nerve was just about to break, when the zombie planted its foot into a pothole in the road. This unexpected jolt shook through the creature's rotten leg, up through its saggy, grey-skinned torso, all the way to its mouldy head, which promptly flew off and tumbled along the floor in front of it. To Melvin's continued astonishment, the body of the zombie **kept on going**. That is, until it tripped over its own detached head, sending its remaining body parts flying in all directions in a final gory flourish.

There was a rattling at the shutters, and it took Melvin a second to realise that it was his shaking hand, gripping the handle of the hatch so tightly that his knuckles had gone white. He actually had to concentrate to relax the muscles in his fingers. Eventually Melvin managed to close the hatch, and he sat in silent contemplation on the floor of the SuperSave. As horrible as what he just witnessed was, he had learned more valuable information about his enemy. The leather shoes, the heat, the deterioration, it could all be used to his advantage, and he knew it. He dusted himself off and went to the clothes section to find himself a leather jacket. It was the first item on a long list of things he would need for his journey to school the next day.

Chapter 9: The school run

Melvin spent the rest of Day Two scouring the SuperSave for useful items. He did this in secret, of course; all too aware that if his mum discovered his plans, he'd be grounded until he was old enough to draw a pension. By the time he was called for tea (tinned spaghetti Bolognese, lovingly prepared in a microwave from the electronics department) he had stashed away the following items:

- 1 pair of black cargo pants (with many pockets for many things)
- 1 black leather jacket (Men's size 'Small'; good job Melvin was tall for his age)
- 1 pair of black leather boots (with steel toes, for kicking)
- 1 set of elbow pads (with added spikes, courtesy of a packet of nails from the DIY department)
- 1 set of shin guards (with the same functional fashion accessories as the elbow pads)
- 10 tins of black shoe polish (a theory of Melvin's; may well put the zombies off even more)
- 1 baseball bat (don't think this one needs explaining)
- 1 axe (nor this one)
- 1 crossbow from the SuperSave 'Outdoor Pursuits' department (ditto)
- 1 quiver of shoe-polish-coated crossbow bolts (getting a bit violent this, isn't it?)
- 1 medical kit (sensible)
- 1 set of walkie-talkies (long range – should reach the school)
- 1 backpack full of food provisions (water, protein bars, and, of course, a tub of *Flobby Jenkins Chocotastic*

Spread)

- 1 pair of black leather gloves (for touching icky things)
- 1 hockey mask (painted black... because it looks cool).

Melvin also made some pretty serious secret modifications to his pedal buggy. By the time he had finished, it had so many stuck-on spikes, protective panels, additional spotlights, mirrors and camouflage nets that it looked like a particularly violent Top Gear challenge.

That evening, as they sat around a garden table, Melvin tried his best to appear positive, cheery and 'normal' to his family. Inside, however, he was fighting a constant battle between fear, and what he knew he had to do to make his family safe. His mum had been trying to call out all day, both on her mobile and the store landline, but all the emergency services were engaged and she couldn't reach any of her friends. She dreaded to think about the possible reasons why – after all... not everyone had an armour-plated supermarket full of supplies to hide in.

Later that night, the McGee family settled into their tented den to sleep. Melvin pretended to nod off first, but kept one slightly-open eye on his mum and his sister. They were all he had left in the world, them and the SuperSave; the constant reminder of his dad's sacrifice. Eventually he allowed his one open eye to slowly close, and he drifted off to sleep.

***

NO! NOt HERE...tHEY Can't aLREaDY BE HERE.

The memory of Mr Plant's frantic warning caused Melvin's entire body to stiffen; fear grabbed hold of him and threatened to squeeze the very breath from his lungs. He couldn't breathe, he couldn't move, all he could do was look down, and as he did, he saw a severed zombie hand crawling across the SuperSave floor, towards his sister. Jessica was still sleeping soundly, completely unaware of the danger that approached. Melvin tried to scream, tried to help, tried to warn his sister, but nothing came out. The hand finally reached Jessica's foot, dragging itself along by its gnarled, rotting fingers, when suddenly it stopped. It twitched. It turned. Then it began scrambling frantically towards Melvin. Clawing its way towards him, it leapt into the air. Melvin could only watch in fear as the grotesque hand plunged its nails into his chest...

BRRRRrrrRRRRrrRRRRRRrRRRrr!

Melvin sat bolt upright in his homemade bed and grabbed his chest, only to feel the vibrations of the silent alarm he had set in his jacket pocket. He was drenched in cold sweat, shivering and breathing hard. It was a dream. It was just a dream. Just a stupid dream. Melvin repeated this calming mantra to himself until he was able to slow his breathing and accept it. He looked around. Jess was just fine, his mum was just fine, he was just fine...

...and it was time for school.

Before leaving the family tent, Melvin slipped one of the walkie-talkies carefully under his mum's pillow. Then, with a last look over his shoulder, he left them and headed towards the main entrance of the store, where the

McGeeMobile (that was what he'd named his modified peddle buggy) awaited, hidden under a sheet of black plastic. Melvin threw off the sheet and checked his provisions. Once he was sure all was present and correct, it was on with the shin pads, elbow pads, jacket, gloves, and of course, the hockey mask. Clambering into the buggy, Melvin peddled slowly and silently towards the main entrance.

He stopped just short of the shutters, got out and approached the mail hatch. He was determinedly confident in his every movement; his hand was sure and steady this time as he reached for the handle. He opened it and peered through – the same scene of destruction and carnage greeted him as yesterday, only with a bit less business-suited-monster. Melvin lingered at the hatch for a good ten minutes, trying to ensure as best he could that the coast was clear. The remote control for the shutters sat in a plastic holder which was mounted to the wall. Having closed the mail hatch, Melvin took it and pressed the green 'up' arrow. The shutters juddered into life, clattering as they dragged themselves off the floor. Melvin wasn't sure which he feared more – attracting the attention of a nearby unseen zombie, or waking his mother and having her discover what he was up to. Thankfully, the gardening department was quite a way from the main entrance, and no zombies came running, so Melvin didn't have to worry about either possibility. Once the shutters were high enough to fit the McGeeMobile under, Melvin returned to his buggy, made his way outside, and pressed the 'down' arrow on the remote.

The shutters closed behind him, and Melvin started to peddle.

Chapter 10: The voice in your head

The summer sun blazed down on Melvin as he trundled cautiously down the street. On any other day, the instant discomfort of being out in hot sunshine while wearing a heavy black leather jacket, black cargo pants, black leather boots and a flipping black hockey mask would have been a major, sweaty issue. On this day, though, the stuffy warmth was a welcome feeling; it felt like a protective shield around our (semi) fearless hero. Plus, he looked totally awesome.

Gradually, Melvin began to pick up speed, taking care to dodge the twisted car parts, branches, bins, broken glass, and, of course, shoes that littered the road. There was no sign of life anywhere. All the windows of the houses were closed and boarded up; all the lights were out. The people of Flinchester were taking the warnings about staying indoors very seriously, and rightly so.

Approaching the first junction, Melvin slowed to a stop, looking around in all directions for movement (and checking in every one of the additional mirrors that he had taped to the frame of the buggy).

"Mirror, signal, move it!" Melvin said to himself as he continued carefully down the road. The further he went, the more devastation he encountered. Telephone poles had been pulled down, broken street lights coughed and spluttered sparks above him, and even as he passed the local park, he could see swings and a slide that had been uprooted and tossed around. Yet there was no sign of the monsters. They really mustn't like the sun, Melvin thought to himself, careful not to let the words out of his mouth this time. As Melvin turned another corner (after the obligatory junction-mirror-check) he passed by the town leisure centre. What he saw made him pull the handbrake hard, sending him skidding violently to a halt, and almost tipping the buggy over in the process.

The leisure centre had large glass windows that ran the full length of the building, so that people could see into the pool area and watch the swimmers and the divers. As Melvin peered through the windows, he could see zombie swimmers – five of them at least – walking down the side of the pool and heading towards the deep end. When they got there, one by one, they jumped in and disappeared under the surface. About halfway down the pool, Melvin saw a decaying zombie head break the surface of the water, moving towards the shallow end. It continued forward, more and more of its rotting body emerging as the water got shallower. When it reached the end, it climbed out, walked the length of the pool, and joined the queue for the deep end.

Melvin realised that the zombies weren't swimming at all: they were jumping in, sinking, and **walking** along the bottom of the pool. He sat and watched them do this for at least five minutes – over and over and over again – and each time they did it, each zombie came out of the pool with another body part missing. Nothing too dramatic, mind; just an ear here and a finger there. They might well have been at this for the last two days, Melvin thought. Old habits really do die hard.

"They aren't stopping, even though they're falling apart!" Melvin whispered to himself.

Just as he was about to leave the scene of this insane parade, he saw one of the zombies break formation and head towards the stairs of the diving board. The board itself was ten metres high – Melvin knew because he and his friends often dared each other to dive-bomb off it. He watched as the zombie climbed all the steps, walked out onto the board and prepared to jump.

Well, it didn't so much jump, as topple, and when it hit the water it didn't so much dive, as explode into a hundred pieces.

Having set off again, Melvin witnessed more mindless zombie routines as he trundled past the local 'Mr Dickens' Finger-Lickin' Chicken' takeout. A gang of infected teenagers stood outside; hoods up, headphones still fixed firmly on their decaying heads. Some had trousers which sagged below their rotting bums; others had lost their pants completely, due to their bottoms having actually dropped off. Yet none seemed to notice; they were all completely focused on the phones in their gnarled, twisted hands. Melvin looked on, puzzled. He could see that all the screens on the devices were black – the batteries must have run out ages ago – yet the zombie teens were still tapping away like mad. No doubt they were trying to beat their high scores on the latest 'Livid Pidgeons' game.

Next door to the takeout was The Flinchester Pub.

Peering through the window, Melvin could see many an overweight, balding zombie 'drinking' from empty pint glasses and moaning something that sounded like football chants at a broken TV. None of them even glanced in Melvin's direction, they were all completely enthralled by the 'game' (which wasn't even on). Melvin then spotted a pair of zombies just to the side of the crowd, playing a game of darts.

He watched as one of the football fanatic zombies walked over, drifting **between** the dart-playing zombies, and stopping just in front of the dartboard. However, the arrival of this clueless creature didn't stop the game; it merely meant that this hapless zombie **became** the dart board. Soon, there were so many darts sticking out of his head, it looked like a zombie pin cushion... and yet, the entire time, he **never** moved an inch. He simply continued to stare at the broken TV, and mumbled something that sounded a bit like 'the referee's a wally'.

Finally it dawned on Melvin. "They are all stuck doing the last thing they did... how weird," he mused as he left this spectacle of barmy behaviour behind.

On the next street, Melvin had to reach under his awesome, intimidating and *totally* necessary hockey mask to hold his nose. The bins from every house had been emptied into the road, and the sun was making everything rot. It **stank**. Melvin sped up slightly, just to escape the smell. He was travelling so fast he almost didn't stop for the next junction. It was only a strange flash of movement in the window of the arcade that stopped him in his tracks.

Melvin wouldn't have stopped if he had thought this was

just another group of zombies doing something mindless and weird, like playing on that claw game where no matter how many goes you have you **NEVER** win **ANYTHING**. You know the one – are those claws covered in butter or something? Seriously, have you ever won **anything** on one of them? Have you ever **seen** anyone win anything? I know your mate probably **told** you that they won a cuddly spider that one time, oh everybody's heard **stories**, but they're **LYING**. Anyway, that's beside the point, because inside the arcade, Melvin could have sworn he saw *human* movement. He'd seen enough over the past couple of days to know the difference. Turning the wheels of the buggy slowly, Melvin peddled towards the arcade for a closer look.

As he approached the entrance, he could see that one of the panels at the bottom of the main door was smashed. The hole was just about large enough for him to fit through, he reckoned. He parked the McGeeMobile and got out, looking in all directions. Carefully, he approached the door, knelt down, and started to crawl through...

"HANG ON A MINUTE! WHat tHE HECK aRE YOU DOInG? YOU'RE On a MISSION!"

...a voice suddenly erupted inside Melvin's head.

He hesitated... the voice was right! What was he thinking? He had a plan, and now he was going to abandon it to venture inside a dark, desolate, potentially zombie-filled arcade? For what? Because he *thought* he saw something? Someone? Yeah right, how about let's get back in the buggy and carry on...

"But what if someone needs help?" Melvin whispered back to the voice in his head.

"YOU NEED HELP! YOU NEED A PSYCHIATRIST IF YOU ARE SERIOUSLY THINKING OF GOING IN THERE! WHO CARES IF SOMEONE NEEDS HELP — YOU NEED TO LOOK AFTER YOURSELF!"

"I - I guess so. I guess you are right." Melvin acquiesced in silence, turning back towards his buggy.

"YEAH I'M RIGHT — NOW DON'T TRY AND BE A HERO — LOOK WHERE THAT GOT YOUR DAD."

Melvin felt an overwhelming sensation of utter disgust and fiery rage. How could he? How could he know that someone might need his help, and just run away? AGAIN!

No, not this time, this time Melvin would ignore the voice in his head, the voice of **FEAR**. He reached into one of his many cargo-pant pockets and took out a tub of black leather shoe polish. Smearing a gunky line under each eye beneath his hockey mask, Melvin felt like a tribal warrior applying war paint. He returned the tub to his pocket. Then, breathing deeply, he lowered himself down and crawled through the jagged hole in the glass.

Emerging on the other side, Melvin felt a sudden, heavy blow to the back of his head, and everything went black.

Chapter 11: Gladys Stickton

It was the strangest feeling... and try as he might, Melvin couldn't get his groggy, aching head around it.

He was lying on his back, he knew that much, and his body was completely numb and motionless. However, he **was** moving along somehow. Through half-closed eyes, Melvin could see a mesmerising haze of blue, green, and orange lights roaming across the sky above him. Then, with a sudden and violent jerk, he was lifted up and launched into what felt like a giant cot made of clouds.

Sinking into the softness, Melvin allowed his droopy eyelids to close once more...

"SORRY I HIT YOU SMELLVIN!"

The booming exclamation caused Melvin's eyes to open wide, although it still hurt too much to move any more of his body than that. He scanned around in an attempt to find the source of the outburst, and a bleary figure suddenly towered over him.

"I thought you were one of THEM! You know, a grabble. Flippin' 'orrible things they are, attacking everybody outside. Can't be too careful can you? That's why me and Gladys had to do what we had to do! No hard feelings, eh SMELLVIN MCWEE?"

There was only one person in the world who called Melvin

McGee 'Smellvin McWee'... and that was **Chloe Barnes**. Chloe was in Melvin's class at school. She was like him, in many ways; lanky, scruffy-haired, and with a slightly chaotic-looking smile. Only she had freckles, too, and a gap between her two front teeth. Melvin hadn't quite decided whether he fancied her or hated her. She was always calling him names, always kicking him then running off, always stealing his pencil case and writing her name on it...

... but she was cute.

Melvin tried to sit up and talk, but the effort proved too much, and he instantly sank back down into the cot made of clouds (which, as it turned out, was a cobbled-together bed made up of cushions from the seats of the arcade restaurant). Melvin decided just to have a go at talking, for now...

"What are you doing here, Chloe?" he managed weakly.

"Well **Smellvin**, I saw that the streets were full of mangy monsters who were grabbing and eating folk, so I decided it would be the perfect time for a game of bowling! What do you think I'm doing here? **HIDING**, you muppet!"

"Alone?" Melvin asked, while trying to stretch out his arms and get some feeling back in his legs.

"Far as I know, 'till **you** showed up of course! Been here for *three* days now! Me and the girls from class skipped school to play laser-tag when the fire alarm went. Everyone else got out, but I got **stuck**! Whose bright idea was it to make the game into a maze, anyway? Idiots! By the time I got out, everyone had scarpered!"

"But how've you survived? The door is smashed in..."

"Yeah, but that's as close as the grabbles have come. For some reason, they don't come inside. Weird, right?"

Melvin craned his sore neck to one side, and as he did so, he saw rows and rows of shiny, leather bowling shoes; there must have been 100 pairs, maybe more.

"Well I think I MIGHT know why they haven't been coming closer! But what have YOU been eating? Aren't you starving?"

"Well, I'm a real Bear Grylls Survival fan, and I've foraged...."

Melvin raised a still-sore eyebrow.

"Hmmmmm, OK, mainly microwaved stuff from the 'restaurant', plus I've pretty much **emptied** one of the vending machines. I've eaten a **LOT** of sugar. I think that's why I got a bit carried away with old Gladys when you poked your daft head through the window!"

Melvin finally managed to sit up, rubbing his stiff neck, with an even more confused look on his face.

"Who's Gladys?"

Chloe nipped behind a rack of bowling balls, then came back wielding the broken handle of a wooden mop.

"Smellvin McWee, meet my friend, **Gladys Stickton.**

"Oh. Oh-kaaaay. It's lovely and completely normal and in no way weird to meet you, Gladys," Melvin replied, even more confused than before.

"She's from **POLE**-land... get it? She's helped me to get a **HANDLE** on the whole situation. We **STICK** together through these tough times!"

Melvin groaned. Even he wasn't sure if it was the pain, or the bad jokes. Maybe it was the bad jokes making the pain even worse. Either way, it was clear that the situation (or the sugar) had sent Chloe a bit bonkers.

"I think you need to come with me." Melvin said authoritatively, lowering his voice to the lowest register he could manage without making his throat hurt as much as his head. "My family is at the SuperSave; we have proper food and supplies. Plus, I have a plan to make everything better... and you can help me."

"Hang on, you want me to go **outside**? Where the grabbles are? Are you completely backwards?"

This seemed like an odd question coming from the girl whose best friend was a broom stick, but Melvin understood her reluctance.

"Trust me, I know how to get around safely. I've been studying the... grabbles... for days now. I made it here didn't I? I can get us both back safe."

Now, Melvin was aware that there were easier, and, let's be

honest, SAFER ways of impressing the perhaps potential girl of his dreams, but those opportunities were, frankly, now a little thin on the ground. Even so, the lady in question didn't seem overly keen on his newest proposition.

"Hmmmmm...

weeeellllllllll...

llleeeeettt...

mmeeeee...

ssseeeeee...

I'm not sure. I'll have to consult my partner!"

Melvin watched as Chloe walked around the rack of bowling balls to talk to her partner, Gladys the stick. He knew he had to get her out of there; she was clearly loopy.

"Okay! We believe you - let's go for it!"

Soon, Melvin and Chloe were making their way to the entrance. Melvin had convinced Chloe to smear shoe polish on herself after he'd explained his leather shoe theory. Chloe had accepted this (mainly due to the evidence of the bowling shoe deterrent) but had demanded some polish, or 'grabble-goo' as she had christened it, for Gladys. The pair (or threesome if you include Gladys) checked that the coast was grabble-clear, then Melvin led Chloe to the McGeeMobile. Chloe stood on the rear axle and hung onto the roof with one hand, while Gladys was held at shoulder height, javelin-style, in the other. Melvin started to peddle back towards the SuperSave.

Chapter 12: Don't Bleed

As they trundled down the road, Chloe's sudden, stunned silence spoke infinitely more than her rapid-fire ramblings in the arcade. She obviously hadn't seen the news, or listened to a radio recently; she had no idea just how bad things were. Now, as Melvin peddled through the wreckage of Flinchester, all Chloe could do was stand on the back of the buggy and stare at the chaos. Melvin could tell how upset she was; Chloe Barnes had **never** gone this long without calling him a name or giving him a dead arm. He turned to offer some words of support, and in doing so, failed to see the shredded tyre which rolled out in front the buggy.

WHAM!

The McGeeMobile was thrown violently up into the air, turned a full and complete circle, and then came down with a heavy thud on the baking concrete. Melvin was OK; he was inside the buggy; all he got for his troubles was a sore bum from landing hard on the plastic seat. Chloe, on the other hand, didn't fare quite so well. She was thrown off the buggy completely, landing in a heap and rolling a good ten feet before coming to a stop, just inches away from a pile of rotting rubbish.

She was **not** pleased.

"**WELL**, THAT'S SOME GREAT DRIVING THERE LEWIS HAMILTON!" she screamed, picking herself up off the floor. "*I CAN GET US BOTH BACK SAFE*, HE SAYS! YOU DRIVE WORSE THAN MY **GREAT GRANDMA**, AND SHE'S **DEAD**! God rest her soul... Now look at this – I'm **bleeding**! Thanks for nothing, **SMELLVIN MCWEE**!"

If this had been any other time, Melvin would have feared the inevitable onslaught of kicked shins, dead arms, and a thousand painful pinches. But right now, what really scared him was the sudden movement he could see.

It was *everywhere*.

"Errrrr... Chloe? I'm really sorry about that, but I think it would be a good idea for you to get back on the buggy... like right now."

"GET BACK ON THAT DEATHTRAP? With Captain Carcrash? No thanks, I think I'd rather walk! In fact, I think I'd still rather walk if the road was covered with broken glass and bogeys! I'd rather walk even if..."

Chloe suddenly stopped complaining, as she, too, noticed the movement all around them. Jumping on the back of the buggy, she shouted just one, much more pertinent word...

"GO!"

Melvin peddled like his life depended on it... because it did. All of a sudden, out of every hiding place, every nook and cranny, every smashed-up car and tipped over wheelie bin, there emerged a ravenous, rotting grabble. They were even more frenzied than before – **way** faster and more animated than Melvin had **ever** seen them. They were closing in on Melvin and his frantic passenger, who continued to scream that one pertinent word, over and over, louder and louder. Melvin was now completely focused, concentrating totally on getting this drive right, as he sent the McGeeMobile skidding around an uncovered manhole. This nifty manoeuvre caught the nearest grabble by surprise, and it fell straight through the open blackness and into the sewers. And yet, even more murderous monsters kept coming. Then, to make matters even worse, Melvin realised they had another, very big, and increasingly immediate, problem.

The security shutters.

The remote only worked close to the shutters, and Melvin knew that even if they got close enough, they wouldn't have the time to wait for the shutters to open before the grabbles caught up with them. There was only one thing for it... it was time to call mum.

"Pass me the walkie-talkie; it's in my back pack!" Melvin yelled over the cacophony of groans and snarls that pursued them. Chloe dug around in the bag and passed him the handset. Melvin pressed the button to connect, and prayed his mum was awake.

"Muuum? Are you there? MUUUUUUUM!"

Funny, what passes through your mind at times like this. Melvin remembered that, when he was a very little boy, his mum always told him that if he got lost in a supermarket, he had to stand still where he was and shout, "MUUUUUUUM!"

Hurtling to the closed entrance of the SuperSave, pursued by a gang of rather angry zombies, Melvin keyed the control button on the handset to connect, and prayed his mum was awake, and would also remember,

"MUUUUM!"

...then an almost desperate,

"MUUUUUUUUUUUUUUUUUUM!"

Static hiss, then, suddenly, the handset burst into life!

"MELBIN! Hello Melbin! Why you on the funny phone?"

"Jessica? Is that you?"

"Where are you Melbeeen?"

"I'm coming back now, Jessy!" Melvin said, trying his best to sound calm. "Put Mum on the funny phone Jess!"

"Okay Melbin! MUUUUM! Melbeeen's on the phone!"

Melvin held his breath, praying silently to hear his mum's voice. Which was pretty impressive, considering that he was also dodging fallen trees, steering round burnt-out cars, and peddling fast enough to stay just in front of the horde of grabbles now chasing them down the road. There must have been thirty, maybe more, and only a few were dropping off now and then (...and by that I mean their legs, arms, or heads, were dropping off now and then). The radio crackled and hissed, then came a very familiar sound...

"MELVIN MARTIN MCGEE!"

That was Melvin's full name, his 'Sunday name' – it only came out when he was in really big trouble. Usually it struck fear into his heart, but right now it was the greatest, most wonderful, most welcome sound he could have hoped to hear.

"Hi mum, it's OK, I mean, I'm OK, but, err, I've done something a bit daft, no time to explain now, but I REALLY need you to open the shutters."

"WHY ON **EARTH** would I open the shutters Melvin?"

"...Because I'm outside."

"YOU ARE **WHERE?**"

Melvin could hear the rage in his mother's voice. It would have terrified him to his core, had he not been in the middle of a chase with monsters who wanted to eat everything except his shoes.

"JUST OPEN THE SHUTTERS MUM! **NOW!**"

The McGeeMobile swerved round the final corner. The SuperSave was straight up ahead... and the shutters were still down.

Melvin continued praying, while peddling faster and faster, trying his best to put some distance between them and the crowd of grabbles. Then he slowed, thinking that if he peddled too fast, his mum might not have time to open the shutters. Chloe screamed again. The radio hissed with static.

Then, just as he was about to give up hope, Melvin saw the shutters twitch. He found another gear in his legs and peddled until smoke started pouring from the front axle. The buggy bounced and swerved round obstacles, while all around them, grabbles began disintegrating – arms and legs and eyeballs started flying everywhere as the monsters struggled to keep up in the hot sun. This just about bought Melvin the space he needed – he launched the buggy over the curb and rocketed through the car park. The shutters came upon him quicker than he anticipated. Melvin instinctively let go of the steering wheel and pulled the handbrake with both hands, sending the McGeeMobile skidding under the shutter and through the main entrance, clattering noisily into a stand full of *Mop-n-Glow* floor polish. Amid the shower of tins hitting the floor, Melvin heard one more, heavier 'thunk' as the shutters closed behind him. He looked round to see his mum with the remote in her hand, and a fearsome look on her face.

"MELVIN MARTIN MCGEE... YOU. ARE. GROUNDED!"

Not a good start. But there's one **other** thing a mum can say that makes you feel worse than anything else. One phrase that they keep tucked away in their back pockets, which only comes out at the direst of moments, when you **really** mess up. As Jane McGee slowed her breathing and approached Melvin, she unleashed that very phrase...

"I'm not angry at you Melvin, I'm just, very **disappointed**."

Melvin fought back burning tears as his mother glared at him. It felt like someone was twisting a knife in his chest. Here he was, trying to make things better, trying to live up to his dad's heroic example, and all he'd managed to do was endanger his family and disappoint his mum.

Well, actually, that wasn't all he'd done. He'd at least managed to help one person. Chloe Barnes stood, shoulder to shoulder, alongside Melvin, as he tried to explain why he had ventured out of the safety of the SuperSave. But Jane was having none of it. She told Melvin that the mad ravings of some loopy caretaker were no reason to leave the store, and that he was lucky to be back in one piece. The only saving grace, she acknowledged, was that he had helped someone else along the way.

"...and who might you be, young lady?" Jane asked as she turned her focus to Chloe. Her voice was softer now, but it still lacked its usual, kind warmth.

"I'm Chloe Barnes, Mrs McGee, and this is my friend Gladys Stickton."

Chloe waved the broken broom handle at Jane. Jane looked back at Melvin, her expression an equal mix of confusion and concern. Melvin simply shook his head and said, "She's been alone for a while. And," he added, sensing a gap to push through, "it was very scary for her out there. All on her own."

"Well Chloe," Jane said, her voice softening further,

"we are glad to have you here, you are safe now."

"Well that's thanks to Smell... I mean Melvin, really. If it wasn't for him, I'd still be stuck in the arcade eating Smarties for breakfast! I know that sounds quite nice, but after a while it makes your teeth hurt!" Chloe smiled, revealing rather alarmingly multi-coloured gums.

Jane remembered her 'mum manners', "First thing's first then, let's get you some proper food. Melvin you stay HERE, and look after Jessica, **got that**?"

"Yes mum." Melvin managed, and he sat down with his sister. As Chloe walked with Jane to the food section, she looked back and gave Melvin a grateful, if rather grotesque, gummy smile.

***

The rest of the day passed without incident – you know how it is when you are in **that much** trouble. Actually, come to think of it, I doubt you have ever been in **that much** trouble. I doubt that you, the wonderfully well-behaved reader, have ever found cause to sneak out of a fortified supermarket to try to save mankind, unintentionally exposing your loved ones to a fate worse than death. But still, you know the "Grounded Ground Rules":
1. Keep your head down.
2. Keep your mouth shut.
3. Keep out of your angry mum/dad/grandma/grandad/teacher/ etc's way.

This 'quiet time' gave Melvin a chance to think about the events of the day, and, in particular, why the zombies were so much more aggressive this time. He was covered in leather, and shoe polish, and the sun was blazing in the sky, yet more grabbles had emerged than ever before ... and they'd all appeared the moment Chloe had...

Blood.

That was it, it had to be! Chloe had been cut when she fell off the buggy. Before that, not one of the grabbles had come anywhere near them. The second Chloe started bleeding, the monsters were drawn to them, and neither the leather nor the sunlight had put them off one bit.

Lesson learned... don't bleed.

Chapter 13: Jailbreak

In Melvin's mind, the plan hadn't changed. It had just become a shedload more difficult.

He knew that they couldn't hole up in the SuperSave forever, watching the country crumble, town by town, on the TVs in the electronics department. He was sure that Mr Plant could help them. At the very least, he knew more about what was going on than anyone else; there was always the hope that he could offer some kind of solution. But how would Melvin escape the SuperSave again, now that his mum, the prison warden, was watching him like a hawk with binoculars? He needed a plan... and a **partner**.

Dawn broke on Day Four of the grabble epidemic. The morning sun streaked through the SuperSave, filling it with the same spidery web of light as yesterday. Only this time, Melvin was already awake, dressed, and slinking silently out of the family tent. This was the only time he could escape his mother's beady-eyed custody long enough to share his plan with his new recruit. He had to make it count.

Padding across the cold, tiled floor in his extra thick socks (specially selected from the clothing department the night before, and perfect for SuperSave sneaking) Melvin approached Chloe's tent. He unzipped the flap just wide enough for him to squeeze through, taking care not to pull the zip too hard in case the noise gave him away. Slowly, carefully, tentatively, he poked his head into the tent...

WHAM!

A splintered piece of wood tore past Melvin's face, grazing the tip of his nose before slamming into the floor. Melvin glanced up to see Chloe towering above him, wielding Gladys Stickton, with a half-asleep, half-furious, fully terrifying look on her face.

"CHLOE! Wait! It's me! Calm down!" Melvin shout-whispered.

You know shout-whispering, don't you? It's that thing you do when you want to scream the place down, but you know that if you do, you'll end up in even bigger trouble than you're already in.

"For goodness sake SMELLVIN! I thought you were one of those monsters! You know how me and Gladys get when we feel threatened!"

Chloe didn't know shout-whispering. Besides, she preferred the more tried-and tested, and, let's face it, more effective whisper-SHOUT.

"SSSHHHH!" Melvin went so far as to flap his hands in front of Chloe's mouth. Not a great life choice, but he survived. "You'll wake mum and Jess up! I need to talk to you, now – it's really important."

Chloe relaxed her grip on Gladys slightly, although she didn't like being shushed and certainly didn't appreciate the hand-flapping bit.

She thought about it, for a second or two, then acquiesced, rather begrudgingly, "...You'd best come in then! Wipe your feet though, I like to keep a clean house."

Melvin did as he was told, then sat and explained all about Mr Plant and his warnings. Chloe couldn't believe that their quiet, unassuming caretaker could have any part in this madness, but she agreed that his actions were so out of character that he may well be hiding something. She could tell from Melvin's honesty and the way he spoke that he meant every word. He wanted to keep his family, and her, safe, and this was the only way he knew how to do it. She knew that to him, safe didn't mean locked up in a fort, waiting for help that might never come. Safe meant finding a **solution** to the problem, like his dad would do. Considering that Chloe also had family out there (at least she hoped they were still out there) she didn't take much convincing. Melvin had his partner, and now it was time to put his plan into action.

Minutes later, Chloe and Melvin were busy in the electronics department, working on part one of the jailbreak master plan. By the time Jessica and Jane started to stir, Melvin was already back in his bed, pretending to be asleep. Chloe was soon back in her own tent, though it took a little longer.

If she was to take part in Melvin's master-plan to defeat the zombies (or hare-brained scheme to get them all killed, as you might also think of it) she had a few essential items on her "to buy" list. So, after a break-neck shopping spree, Chloe was packing the following for her trip of a lifetime:

MORGUE

SO Miami Vice, daahling
1 leather jacket *(women's size small, with the sleeves rolled WAY up)*.

For that battlefield to office look
1 pair of cargo pants *(with half the pockets filled with shoe polish, and the other half filled with plasters)*.

Stilettos are so "last year"
1 pair of leather boots *(same steel toes, for the same maximum kickability)*.

Think Jody Kidd on the grid, not the catwalk
2 pairs of elbow pads *(to wear one on top of the other, just in case 'Captain Crash' bins the buggy again)*.

2 pairs of shin guards *(more tarmac protection) If it's good enough for the England ladies' footy team, it's good enough for Chloe Barnes!*

Fashion accessories
1 roll of black electrical tape, and 1 pack of nails. Proper "hammer and nails" not stick-ons, extensions or falsies. *(Fashion accessories for Gladys Stickton)*.

1 pair of leather gloves lined with cashmere *(natch)* for better grip when swinging Gladys.

1 backpack full of supplies *(including snack bars, water, and more plasters: thou shalt not bleed)*. Forget all of the "pack light" advice, girls, this time, think "pack fight".

This year's "must have" accessory
1 hockey stick *(courtesy of the sporting goods section, and aptly named 'Mr Glen Stickton')*.

1 pointy-horned devil mask *(from the dressing up section, strictly for intimidation purposes)*.

Chloe had stashed all this gear, along with Melvin's supplies, near the McGeeMobile, which still sat at the main entrance amongst a pile of *Mop-n-Glow* floor polish.

After hearing Jane calling her for breakfast, she eventually emerged from her tent, stretching and yawning, playing her part perfectly. As they sat round the table eating bowlfuls of Choco-Flakes, the mood was much lighter than the previous day. Jane even smiled at Melvin across the table and told him how glad she was that he was safe and sound. She explained that she understood his efforts to help the family, even if they had frightened the living bejaysus out of her. She also told him about the reports on the news that morning, and how it said that some of the families stuck indoors in Flinchester were starting to get low on food. She spoke about how lucky they were to have all the supplies they could need, thanks to their dad. But it was her next words that really twisted the knife in Melvin's chest.

"We all just need to sit tight right here, where it's safe. That's why your dad brought us here, it's what he would have done."

Melvin gritted his teeth and forced a smile, gulping down the lump in the back of his throat. He knew this *wasn't* what his dad would have done. His dad was a **problem solver**; he always made things better, and things were not going to get better if they just sat around the SuperSave and waited. It was time for part two of the master plan.

After breakfast, Melvin and Chloe went off to the toy section to play... at least that's what they told Jane McGee they were doing. Every so often, Jane would walk by the entrance of the toy department to check on them, and would hear them arguing over whose turn it was to play Ninja Octopus 2: The Inking, or who got to be the blue Ravenous, Ravenous Rhino. On her fourth patrol, Jane was surprised to hear the pair *still* arguing about whose turn it was to 'kill the mutant squirrel boss on level 6', so she popped her head around the entrance of the toy section. There, in the middle of the aisle, was a laptop, connected to a set of speakers, playing a looped recording of two children arguing over a computer game...

Melvin and Chloe were nowhere to be seen.

***

"WATCH OUT FOR THAT BIN LID!"

"CAREFUL OF THAT TREE!"

"LOOK OUT! SHOES!"

Chloe was, understandably, a tad nervous about Melvin's driving. After gearing up and sneaking out of the SuperSave, they had already reached the swimming pool, and even though there had been no sign of the grabbles, the fear of Melvin's motoring skills were enough to put her on edge. Melvin, for his part, was actually concentrating very hard on his driving, for three reasons. Firstly, the whole attempting to avoid death thing, secondly, to keep Chloe happy (or as happy as a frantic, stick-wielding nutter can be), and thirdly, because it distracted him from the horrible feelings of guilt caused by having to deceive and worry his mother, again.

Having braved Hold Your Nose Road and passed Chloe's arcade, Melvin brought the buggy to a slow, careful stop at the next junction.

"Why are we stopping Melvin?" Chloe asked, in a voice that was slightly too loud for comfort.

Melvin didn't say anything, he didn't even look at her. He simply stared forward, and nodded his head, gesturing for her to look down the road. There, in the forecourt of the *Gleam Sheen* car wash, was a team of boiler-suited grabbles. Some stood chewing on soapy sponges, others were snacking on tree-shaped air fresheners. One even had a hose pipe in his mouth, chugging water, which subsequently spurted out of several holes in his torso and made him look like a giant garden sprinkler.

"They look hungry," whispered Chloe, all of a sudden extremely aware of the volume of her voice.

"Mmhmm," agreed Melvin, equally quietly. "Grotty, rotten swines - let's see just how hungry they are..."

Melvin began to peddle again; slowly, but purposefully. He readied himself to peddle like crazy if necessary, but for now he held his nerve, and his speed, nice and steady. As they approached the garage, one of the nearest grabbles looked up from his soapy sponge sandwich and sniffed in their direction. A look of pure disgust spread across its already repulsive, rotting face, and just as quickly, it returned to its revolting lunch.

"It's working, the leather and goo is working! You're a genius!" Chloe whispered, with equal parts excitement and

relief.

Again, Melvin said nothing. He simply peddled on, focused and determined. Soon they neared Flinchester Zoo, which meant that they were getting close to Green Oaks Primary School. However, as they passed the zoo, Melvin was compelled to slow the buggy to a stop again. Only this time, it wasn't what he *saw*, but rather, what he *heard*.

If you consider the horrible things Melvin had witnessed over the preceding days, you might be shocked to hear that this sound, emanating from the very bowels of the zoo, struck the most fear into him of anything yet. It was a **dreadful** noise, an **unnatural** noise, a noise that sent cold, spiking shivers right through Melvin, and left him wanting nothing more than a place to hide away until it ceased. At first, it sounded like feral animals howling in a mix of pain and anger. Then it seemed to change, rising and building, not animal, not human, but something else. It was the dire chant of desperate, ravenous, disturbed souls... and it was **truly** terrifying.

"I think we need to get going Melvin... please," Chloe managed. She was just as frightened by the sound as Melvin was.

Melvin began to peddle again, slowly. It took them the entire length of two more long, winding streets to escape the appalling sound completely, by which point they had arrived at a set of green iron gates, above which was a sign that read,

WELCOME TO
GREEN OAKS PRIMARY SCHOOL

Chapter 14: Petrov Larnt

Melvin came to a careful halt, and Chloe released her white-knuckled grip on the frame of the McGeeMobile, stepping cautiously down from the rear axle. Eyes darting back and forth, watching for the slightest hint of grabble movement, she crept towards the gates and pushed them open. Melvin began to peddle through, and Chloe hopped back on as the buggy trundled down the wide path to the main entrance of the school.

The place was in ruins. Almost every window was broken; doors hung from their hinges; walls were blackened in places where fire had engulfed parts of the building. Melvin could only hope that all this damage had been done after the initial attack. A sudden pang in his chest made it hard for him to breathe as he thought about his friends. This was the last place he had seen them, on the morning of his birthday, when they had greeted him with cheers and a Happy Birthday banner.

That felt like a million years ago. And Melvin felt an awful lot older.

Melvin tried to concentrate on peddling around the debris that carpeted the concrete path. Lunchboxes, book bags, pencil pots, trays with children's names on; each obstacle was a fresh reminder that so many people had been affected by the outbreak. A sudden gust of wind breezed through the school building, swirling in and out of broken windows, picking up and carrying with it a fresh collection of mementos to be cast out onto the path. A yellow maths book landed square in Melvin's lap; he turned it over and read the name 'Scotty Parkinson' on the cover; Melvin's best friend. He handed the book to Chloe, instructing her to put it in his rucksack. Chloe was about to question why when she read the name on the front. She opened the bag in silence and stashed the book away. Eventually, they reached the end of the path, which opened up on to the playground. There, on the far side of the yard, stood Mr Plant's office.

Melvin parked the McGeeMobile just outside the office, and the pair collected their more 'defensive' supplies from the luggage compartment. Chloe hung Glen the Hockey Stick from a loop on her back pack, then grabbed Gladys Stickton. Melvin put on his backpack too, then looped the shoulder straps of his crossbow and quiver of bolts over his head. Finally, he picked up his, as yet, un-named baseball bat, Chloe having bagged the best aliases for her weapons. Together the pair ventured towards the office. It looked like one of those mobile cabins you see on building sites, with a single door and wire cages over the windows. You know, the ones inhabited by teams of plump men, who sit and drink tea while discussing the possibility of the chance of considering thinking about doing some work, maybe. It was a pretty secure, well-protected building and, now Melvin came to think about it, very apt for someone who might be expecting a zombie attack. Melvin reached out to try the handle. It was unlocked. Maybe not so safe after all. He used the end of the bat to push the door open slowly. It creaked on its hinges, opening inch by inch to reveal...

A chair.

Not just any chair, mind you, but one of those big comfy

swivel ones. There was also a desk, which was extremely tidy, and a noticeboard filled with rotas and forms. There were filing cabinets, stationery pots, even a little fridge. But there was no Mr Plant.

Not exactly sure what he was looking for, Melvin scoured the walls for clues that Mr Plant was indeed someone who knew what was going on. But there was nothing, nothing scientific... no equipment that was out of place for a caretaker, no proof that he was someone who could help in any way, for that matter. Chloe followed Melvin in and closed the door behind her. She was quick to voice her opinion.

"Well, this was a wonderful waste of time, wasn't it Smellvin? Properly glad I risked my life coming all the way here so that I could admire Mr Plant's office. Just the sight of this stationery set makes me feel **soooo** good about almost **dying**."

Melvin had nothing to say, he simply dropped to his knees and lowered his head. He felt hopeless. This was it; his whole plan had hinged on this place, and there was nothing there. He was done.

"Well since I'm here, I might as well indulge in the lavish luxuries of Mr Plant's dwelling. Heaven knows I wasn't comfy enough in my own safe, pillow-filled tent in the SuperSave, here I get to enjoy this amazing CHAIR! I might just go nuts and raid his fridge, too!"

Chloe reached down and opened the mini fridge. To her surprise it was empty, except for an odd, black box at the back of the top shelf. She took it out and inspected it; it had a single, red button on the top. On it was printed words like "Danger", "Be careful", and "Do not press unless really, really certain".

"Melvin, have a look at this. I wonder what it is..."

Melvin looked up from the ground. Of course, Chloe had pressed the red button. Behind them both, a square metre of floor in the middle of the office fell away with a clang, revealing a deep, black, cavernous opening. Melvin and Chloe leapt back in shock, and as they did, the hole seemed to illuminate from the bottom up. Melvin crawled towards the edge and peered down. The shaft was about 10 metres deep, and a metal ladder, attached to one of its walls, descended into the shadows.

"I knew it," Melvin said under his breath.

Chloe stood behind Melvin and peered over him, looking straight down the shaft.

"So, our caretaker is actually Bruce Wayne?" she said, shaking her head in disbelief. "Well, this day just gets madder and madder!"

Energised by this new discovery, Melvin descended the ladder, and Chloe followed close behind. They reached the bottom, turned, and both of their mouths dropped open in unison. There, sprawling out in front of them, was a science lab full of complicated equipment. Racks of test tubes filled with different colour liquids lined the walls. Bottles and jars connected by a labyrinth of pipes covered two large tables in the middle of the room. Giant oven-like contraptions with skull-and-crossbones stickers stood at one end of the room, while at the other there was a desk and a noticeboard. Unlike the desk above, this one was a total mess, covered in hastily scrawled notes and photocopied pages from very complicated-looking books. The noticeboard, far from being filled with rotas and forms, displayed a collection of newspaper articles, the headlines of which suddenly made things a whole lot clearer for Melvin...

PETROV LARNT AWARDED PRESTIGIOUS SCIENCE PRIZE

SCIENTIST PETROV LARNT PIONEERS NEW GENETIC FOOD BREAKTHROUGH

'TOO MUCH, TOO SOON' LARNT WARNS

SCIENTIST DISAPPEARS AMID GENETICS ROW

While Melvin stood, taking all of these revelations in, Chloe had begun to look through the drawers in the desk. She pulled out a handful of documents and started rifling through them.

"Hey, there's a passport here... and another one! Have a look Melvin."

Chloe opened one, while Melvin inspected the other. One was written in a foreign language, it looked Russian, yet the person in the photo ID was definitely Mr Plant. Or, as he was named in the passport, '**Petrov Larnt**'.

"This one is a British passport – I've got one just like it," said Melvin as he opened his up to the photo page. Sure enough, there was the same photograph, only this time identified as '**Trevor Plant**'.

UNITED KINGDOM of GREAT BRITAIN and NORTHERN IRELAND

SURNAME:
PLANT   PASSPORT NUMBER
                         234634876
GIVEN NAMES:
TREVOR

NATIONALITY:
BRITISH CITIZEN

DATE OF BIRTH:
21. 1. 1964

"So Mr Plant isn't a caretaker at all. Or at least he wasn't. Look at the names,"

Melvin pointed back to name in the foreign passport,

P-E-T-R-O-V L-A-R-N-T

Then Melvin held up the other passport next to it, comparing the name.

"Switch the letters around, look what happens. Petrov Larnt becomes..."

"**Trevor Plant**! Flipping heck, the plot thickens!" Chloe replied.

"I **knew** he was something to do with it! Look at these news stories. They were experimenting with food. Looks like he saw trouble ahead, but no-one would listen to him..."

Melvin was stopped in his tracks, as suddenly all the lights in the lab went out. Only the entrance to the shaft remained lit up, and Melvin and Chloe wasted no time hurrying over to the ladder. But, just as they began to climb, the lid above them slammed shut, sending the whole place into complete blackness. The pair froze halfway up the ladder, panicking. Then they heard a sound. *That* sound. The **sound from the zoo**. Only this time, it was **in the room**. It rose and rose until it became almost deafening. Then, just as quickly, it stopped, only for a single, rumbling voice to take its place...

"YOU SHOULD NOT HAVE COME HERE!"

...and with that, Melvin and Chloe were pulled, screaming, into the darkness.

Part 3: The Sacrifice

Chapter 15: Zee Truth

In reality, Melvin and Chloe couldn't have spent more than a few seconds clawing and screaming in the pitch-black void. Yet, to the terrified pair, it felt like time itself stood still, just so it could watch them suffer. They shivered, they cried, Melvin even let out a whimpering "Mummy!" at one point. Chloe might have, too, but she wouldn't admit it. And yet, almost as quickly as they had been plunged into darkness, the room was suddenly filled with bright white light, and a maniacal sound...

HAAHΣΣHAꓤꓤ!

HAHAHΣΣAHAꓤ!

Melvin squinted, his eyes struggling to adjust to the brightness. His vision was a blur of white shapes and patchy, intermingled colours. Focusing on the direction of the sound, he slowly made out the shape of a person. A man.

It was Mr Plant.

He was stood in the archway of a hitherto-unseen door, concealed at the back of the room. The laughter was his... and he was **still** going.

"Haahahaaaa! Ohhhh! I have not had zee laughs like zis in years! You should haff seen your faces! Vot a peek-ture!"

Chloe rubbed her eyes with one hand and instinctively felt around the floor for Gladys with the other. Melvin grabbed her arm and indicated towards the back of the room. Looking up, Chloe suddenly felt the need to rub her eyes even harder...

"Mr Plant?" she managed, eventually.

"Ah come now, vee both know zat iz not my real name! I saw you doing zee sneaking and zee snooping! My name iz Petrov Larnt... **Doctor** Petrov Larnt!"

"Why are you talking funny?" Chloe asked, still straining to see in the brightness.

"Zis iz how I **really** sound, my young friend! I am from **Russia**!"

The whole scene was starting to resemble an audition from X Factor, so Melvin did a "Simon" and cut to the chase.

"I thought you were from Flinchester! You've talked like us ever since you started here!"

Mr Plant... sorry, Dr Larnt nodded enthusiatically: "Vell... ven von adopts a new identity, von must make it convincing, yes? I vorked hard to blend in here in Flinchester, to go unnoticed vile I completed my vork."

At the sound of this, Melvin piped up,

"What **work**, Doctor Larnt? What have you been doing here? You know about the zombies, don't you?"

"Know about zem? Dear boy... I knew about zem **months** ago. Take a seat, both of you. Zere iz much to discuss..." Dr Larnt gestured grandly with his right hand for the two of them to sit down.

Doctor Larnt proceeded to fill in the gaps in what Melvin and Chloe already knew. He had indeed been a genetic scientist, and a very successful one at that. He had been paid a vast sum of money by a food company to experiment on chickens in an attempt to make them both tastier and healthier to eat.

He succeeded in doing this, but the company that employed him did not stop there. First, they demanded that he make the chickens **bigger**, so they could harvest more meat. Larnt had reluctantly agreed to this, and the result was a new, classified breed of chicken, which stood over five-feet tall. Next, the company wanted Larnt to modify the eating habits of the chickens, turning them into cannibalistic carnivores which would eat leftover parts of **other** chickens. This would, in turn, make them even bigger, and would also cut down on waste costs. Larnt had warned that any more modification could have disastrous consequences for the humans who ate these chickens, but the company would not listen. Doctor Larnt was fired, and other scientists in his team continued these unnatural, hazardous, and potentially deadly experiments.

Before leaving the company, Larnt had managed to sneak a look at the organisation's private plans. It was then that he learned that the first human trials for chicken taste-testing were scheduled to take place in just over half a year, at a large testing facility in Miltington, England.

So, with a forged passport and a new accent, the newly named 'Trevor Plant' applied for a caretaker job at a school in Flinchester, a neighbouring town. There, he would be far enough from the testing facility not to be recognised by the workers, but close enough to monitor the facility, and act if his dire predictions came true.

Trevor had arranged for his mobile cabin to be placed in a very specific part of the playground, which gave him access to the sewer system underneath the school. He had then spent the first month clearing enough space for a lab, and the next month smuggling in science equipment. After that, it was down to work, trying to find a way to reverse the changes that he predicted the modified chicken would cause. It was all going well until that fateful day, when he read in the paper that taste-testing for a new variety of chicken was already underway at the facility. He was too late to stop the outbreak, but he had not given up completely. That very morning, just before Melvin and Chloe had turned up, he had finally completed his work... he had created a cure.

"Vud you like to see it?" The doctor asked, already turning away and heading towards what looked like a giant freezer. Melvin and Chloe sat, dumbfounded, trying to process everything that they had heard. Melvin knew one thing, though, he was right. He'd found a way to save his family, everything was going to be OK.

He was also immensely pleased to have found an adult who
1. At least SEEMED to have a handle on the situation
2. Was keen to help Melvin as much as Melvin needed to be helped.
3. Hadn't tried to eat Melvin or his friend. Always a plus.

"Here vee are – my masterpiece!" Melvin tuned back into Dr Larnt again.

Doctor Larnt held up a thin steel cylinder. It was about three inches long, slightly thicker than a medical syringe, with tiny, glass panels that ran all the way round the sleek, silver tube. These panels revealed the contents: a peculiar, gungy liquid which seemed to glow as it sloshed from side to side. It was red; a vibrant, sharp red; the colour of fresh blood, and it contained tiny flecks of blue, luminous, crystal-like pieces. These fragments zipped around, crashing into the glass panels and bouncing off again, making it look like the contents were in perpetual motion. The cylinder itself tapered into a very sharp point at one end, which raised a question that Chloe was all too ready to ask...

"What's the pointy bit for?"

"Vell, you see, zis is vot vee call a '**RETROVIRUS**'. Zat means it is a virus, like a bug or an illness, but vee use it to fight **anozer** virus, like zee one zat is spreading around zis country like zee vild fire. Like any virus, it needs a **carrier**. In ozer vords, vee need to INJECT it into von of zose infected... things."

"INJECT IT?" Chloe started up, "I'm sorry, but I think you'll struggle for volunteers who want to get close enough to one of those things to give them a flipping injection! Besides, me and Melvin are scared of needles, allergic, in fact, aren't we, Mel...." she tailed off when she saw Melvin's set, studious expression.

"Yes... it vill be quite problematic." Larnt acknowledged. "Especially as I really need to target von of zee carriers in particular – zee first von who vas infected, zee von who brought zee infection to Flinchester..."

"...Mr Woods," said Melvin, almost to himself.

"Yes indeed! Top marks! Your teacher vas a volunteer taste tester; zee first. If he is injected, zee retrovirus vill spread more quickly. It is zee most effective vay. If vee target him, zen no matter vot has happened to zee ozer zombies, no matter how many parts zay are missing, new limbs vill sprout, new parts vill form, and zay vill be fine!"

Chloe shook her head in disbelief, partly at what Larnt was saying, partly at his accent. "Let's assume you can even find anyone bananas enough to get that close to a grabble, how would they ever find Mr Woods? He could be **anywhere!**"

"Zat is not a problem! I haff eyes everywhere!" Larnt exclaimed as he returned the cylinder to the gigantic fridge.

"Why did I just KNOW he was going to say that?" Chloe said, quietly. Larnt headed over to a bank of computer screens on the far wall. With a few mouse clicks and pushed buttons, all the screens illuminated, filled with images from security cameras all over town. One screen in particular showed Flinchester Zoo, and with the image came that awful sound once again, throbbing through speakers and filling the lab.

"HE'S GONE TO THE ZOO?! WHAT, DID HE FANCY A ZOMBIE DAY OUT OR SOMETHING?" Chloe shouted over the horrendous din.

"Much vorse, I'm afraid," said the doctor as he muted the sound. "Haff a look – he has taken over zee zoo... and he iz not alone."

Melvin and Chloe ignored the annoying realisation that it was **this** sound recording that the Doctor had used to scare them, and instead they studied the screen. It showed a live feed (excuse the pun) from the ape house at the zoo. But there were no apes. There were **parts** of apes, here and there, but the cages that used to house them had been torn open and emptied. The whole place was a wreck, and the only inhabitants left were a horde of zombies, scrambling, clambering and crawling all over the entire enclosure. In the middle, sat on a pile of rocks above all the others, was Mr Woods.

"What is he? Like... King of the Grabbles?" Chloe spluttered.

"Apparently so! I haff monitored zem for zee past few days. Zee other zombies, zay bring him food, zey chant for him, and zey follow his orders. Zey are... hiz **army**."

"Well, that'll be that then! No-one is getting anywhere

near close enough to inject him. It's game over man. Game over!" Chloe was almost shouting again.

"Yes... I assumed az much. But I haff just had anozer brilliant idea!" said the doctor, his eyes suddenly lighting up as he eyed Melvin's crossbow.

"Are you a good shot vith zat, Melvin?" he asked, hopefully.

"I **will** be. Trust me." Melvin replied, a sudden look of determination on his face.

"Right zen! We don't need to get close, just close *enough*. Let's get planning! Zee people of Flinchester need us – I haff been watching zee news – families are getting low on food. Vee need to act now, while zere are still people left to save!"

"Yay! Let's do it! Let's save the town! Goooooo TEAM!" Chloe exclaimed, only a tad sarcastically, punching the air in victory.

Or at least she had **intended** to punch the air. The problem was, she didn't check (as one doesn't) that the space above her head was actually filled with **air**. It wasn't. It was filled with a rack of glass test tubes which hung from the wall behind her. There was an almighty crash above her, an almighty howl from her mouth, and, when she brought her hand back down, an almighty torrent of blood flowing from a cut across her knuckles.

Melvin stared at her hand, the colour draining from his face as fast as it was draining from Chloe's knuckles.

"Oh no," he whispered...

"...blood."

Chapter 16: Give us a hand

Doctor Larnt turned even paler than Melvin. He also knew how dangerous even a tiny drop of blood in the air was. Darting across the room, he ripped a first aid kit off the wall and rifled through it until he found a roll of bandage. He began furiously winding it around Chloe's hand, layer upon layer, in an attempt to stop the bleeding and mask the scent.

But it was too late.

GRRRRRRROOOOOWW WWWWRRRRRR!!!

That noise. That dreadful noise, back again. It grated like fingernails on a chalkboard, accompanied by an orchestra's-worth of out-of-tune violins, played by drowning cats. It was bad, is what I'm saying, and what was worse was that the speakers in the lab were turned off...

It was coming from above.

"Vee haff to get out of here! NOW!" cried the doctor, as he frog-marched the pair towards the hidden door at the back of the room, stopping only to grab the precious cylinder from the fridge. Furious footsteps hammered on the ceiling above them, sending dust from cracks in the roof cascading down all over the shiny lab equipment.

It sounded like there were hundreds of them up there already.

"Qvickly, children, it iz only a matter of time before zey break open zee trap door. Follow me... zis vay!"

Larnt put his full weight into the heavy door and shoulder-barged it open, then he ushered Melvin and Chloe through and forced it closed again. Having pulled a torch from one of the many pockets of his labcoat, the doctor illuminated the sewer pipe they had entered. Pausing briefly, they heard the trapdoor in the lab behind them break open. The terrorised trio turned and started sprinting down the tunnel; they dared not think about what they were stepping in as they sloshed and splashed through the stinky sewers. They simply ran, as far and as fast as they could. Eventually they came to a metal ladder, which led up to a manhole cover, which would in turn take them back to the surface.

"Here, Chloe, let me look at your hand," the doctor said, inspecting Chloe's wrapped knuckles under the torchlight. The bleeding had stopped, and none of the blood had seeped through.

"Vee should be safe now, and if my memory iz correct, zis ladder should bring uz out just across zee road from zee zoo!"

The doctor shone his light on the ladder, allowing Melvin and Chloe to start climbing. At the top of the ladder, Melvin pushed his shoulder into the heavy, metal manhole cover, creating a gap just big enough for Chloe to jam Glen Stickton into. Melvin then used the hockey stick as a lever to slide the manhole cover to one side, giving them enough room to get out. Melvin escaped first, taking care to look around for grabble movement before giving Chloe the all-clear. Just as she managed to clamber free, Melvin heard a low sound, a sound that he hoped they had left behind. It seemed to be getting louder... and closer...

"Err... Doctor Larnt? I think I hear something... and I think you should hurry."

"Yes, my dear boy, I'm on my vay, fear not!"

Melvin sighed with relief as the gruesome sound stopped just as suddenly as it had started. He saw the doctor's arm emerge from the grid, the canister clutched tight in the palm of his hand, and Melvin's half smile returned...

KRRUUUNCHHHH.

A sudden, sickening sound echoed from the sewers, and Melvin's smile instantly disappeared.

"Doctor?"

"Doc?"

"Are you OK Doctor Larnt?" Chloe squeaked, peering tentatively over the edge of the manhole. Melvin was shocked to see her turn away suddenly, a look of utter disgust and terrifying shock on her face as she started to run.

"Chloe! Chloe **wait**! ...Doctor Larnt?"

Melvin ventured closer, staring at the doctor's unmoving hand. As he approached the manhole, he craned reluctantly to peer down the shaft. There was Doctor Larnt's arm. But as for the rest of him? It was nowhere to be seen.

Melvin had to cover his mouth to stop himself from throwing up on the spot. This battle against the spew only worsened when he realised he'd have to take the canister from Larnt's hand before it slipped back into the sewer. Kneeling down, and trying not to look, he prised the delicate canister from the doctor's fingers and backed away, his eyes darting all around as he retreated. But the zombies didn't come out of the sewer and into the sunlight. They didn't grab Melvin. His leather and polish protection was still working. It was just a terrible shame that the same could not be said for the good doctor.

"CHLOE!" Melvin shout-whispered as he scanned around for his partner, taking care not to draw too much attention to himself. As Melvin manoeuvred carefully around an upside down car, he discovered his partner sat behind it, her knees drawn up to her chest, her face buried in her hands.

"Chloe... are you OK?"

Chloe looked up at Melvin, and Melvin saw something that he had never seen before. Chloe Barnes was crying. Chloe Barnes **never** cried. She kicked you, called you names, stole the biscuits from your lunchbox and gave you dead arms. She even flicked bogeys at you if you really upset her, but she **NEVER** cried.

"I...miss...my...mum!" Chloe managed, between sobs.

Melvin wasn't sure if he'd get a punch for trying, but he knelt down beside Chloe and put his arm round her. To his surprise, she tucked her head under his arm, and cried even harder.

"I didn't...want...to say...a-a-anything," Chloe snivelled, wiping her nose on her sleeve. "After what... h-happened to your dad, I didn't want to... complain."

Melvin felt truly awful. All this time he'd been so fixated on his family and his sadness, and so used to Chloe being so funny and so confident, that he'd almost forgotten that she had family out there too... somewhere.

"It's going to be OK Chloe. I promise. Look what I have..."

Melvin opened his hand and showed Chloe the vial that contained the cure. With a sniff and a wipe of her nose, Chloe smiled through her remaining tears.

"Oh, that's just grand. Peachy, in fact. So I guess it's just a case of taking on Woodsy and his grabble army now, eh?"

Melvin smiled too.

Well, half-smiled.

"Yup... and I couldn't have picked a better teammate for the job."

"Don't be getting all mushy on me now SMELLVIN, that will do us **no** good... **in there**."

Chloe nodded upwards, to a sign that hung above a large, chain link fence. It read,

FLINCHESTER ZOOLOGICAL PARK

"Well, I was actually talking about Gladys," Mevin said through a crooked smirk, nudging Chloe in the side. "Now come on, no time to waste, is there?"

The pair got to their feet, dusted themselves off, and began to walk towards the main entrance of the zoo. As he approached the gates, Melvin thought about how far he'd come. The birthday breakfast table seemed like a lifetime ago, and yet, in reality, only a few days had passed. It's like the old saying goes, I suppose; one minute you are eating toast with your age written on in jam, the next you are taking on a zombie hoard with a frizzy-haired maniac and a talking stick.

Growing up can be so weird. Ah well, there were always the teenage years to look forward to.

Chapter 17: Grabbanimals

Chloe and Melvin paused just short of the grand iron gates which hung, broken and twisted, at the entrance to the zoo. Melvin set down his backpack, and Chloe followed suit. Layers of grabble goo were then liberally applied, extra plasters were stuck all over Chloe's knuckles, shin pads and elbow pads were tightened, and totally scary face masks were donned. Then came the most important part of the preparation.

Melvin selected one of the crossbow bolts from the quiver which hung over his shoulder. He unscrewed and removed the pointed tip, took the vial which contained the cure and pushed the end of the shaft into the bottom of the cylinder. The fit was almost right, but the vial wobbled slightly, so Melvin delved back into his backpack and pulled out a roll of the same duct tape he had used all over the McGeeMobile. He wrapped it round and round, over the join between the shaft and the tube, until it was as secure as he could possibly make it. Melvin also doubled up some tape and wrapped it around the bottom of the bolt, near the flight, so it was sticky to the touch. It was all a bodge-job, but it was the best he could manage, and it would have to do. With backpacks re-packed, Gladys and Glen at the ready, and the cure bolt safely stashed back in the quiver, Melvin and Chloe ventured into the zoo.

The grabbles had really done a number on the place. The total and utter destruction that sprawled out in front of Chloe and Melvin made the rest of Flinchester look like a number one tourist destination: a 'Britain in Bloom' winner, ten years in a row. The remains of three refreshment stands stood smouldering in the heat; the sickly-sweet smell of scorched sugar still hung in the air. In the middle of a grassy picnic area, a tall, wooden giraffe stood, swaying in the summer breeze on its one remaining leg, with a splintered sign that read 'Sloth's Smoothie Stall' swinging from its nose. At least a dozen metal bars, which had been ripped from ticket turnstiles, now protruded from walls and fences. Bins had been emptied out; windows had been smashed; doors had been ripped off hinges; barely anything remained untouched or undamaged. But none of this interested Melvin and Chloe.

They were too busy looking at the tiger.

That's right, a tiger. A dirty-great-big, man-eating tiger. It was sat at the far end of the picnic area, sunning itself in the afternoon heat, being all tigery and massive and deadly. It hadn't noticed Melvin and Chloe... yet.

Whilst struggling to ensure that the contents of their stomachs didn't make a rapid and undignified emergency exit from either possible direction, Chloe and Melvin came to a very unsettling realisation. The animals of Flinchester Zoo were no longer caged attractions. They were now yet another threat to add to the pair's already substantial list. Thankfully, the path to the ape house lay in the opposite direction.

"This way!" Melvin whispered as he gestured towards the path. "I'd rather end up a zombie than tiger poop!"

Without taking their eyes off the tiger, the pair began to back away. Melvin never thought he'd be happy to be heading **towards** a nest of ravenous zombies. Funny how things work out...

Once well clear of the picnic area, the pair turned and padded carefully along the path. The hairs on Melvin's neck bristled; he could feel movement everywhere. Every tree they passed seemed to writhe and squirm with life. Peering closer, Melvin spotted snakes wrapped around the tree trunks, wild birds perched in udulating rows, even the odd small monkey swinging from branch to branch. It was deeply unsettling. But Melvin knew the zoo well, and he knew that there was a greater danger ahead, and it wasn't the grabble hangout. Before they even got to that part, they would have to pass the **lion enclosure**. There was no other way, thanks to the sunbathing tiger. But what if the lions were on the loose too? Melvin wasn't sure that **they** were so particular when it came to the taste of leather and shoe polish.

Slowly, cautiously, Melvin and Chloe passed under a grand, wooden arch, with a sign displaying the words '**AFRICAN PREDATORS - The Lion's Lair**'. Until now, this had been Melvin's favourite part of the zoo. He knew all there was to know about the biggest lion that lived there. His name was 'Lenny', he was bred in captivity, he was twelve years old, he weighed 200 kilos and he measured just over three metres from head to tail. Checking these facts off in Melvin's mind proved a temporarily useful distraction, until he realised that three metres was twice his height, and 200 kilos was more than four times his weight. That, PLUS a mouth full of large, very pointy teeth, plus the fact that the aforesaid animal might well be enjoying unaccustomed freedom to wander around the zoo, equalled a very dodgy tummy situation for Melvin.

And what he saw as he approached Lenny's enclosure didn't quite settle his tummy, so much as send a Richter-scale-busting earthquake tremoring through it.

Melvin's attention was immediately grabbed by a gruesome, fly-infested, rotting pile of odd, lumpy shapes, stacked in the far corner. Melvin soon figured out what the lumps were. It will hopefully be enough to say that it was a pile of 'spare monkey parts', and leave the rest to your doubtlessly plenty-gross imagination. Melvin turned away in disgust. It was definitely a "Shouldn't Have Gone to Specsavers" moment. Melvin scanned across the rest of the enclosure, only to spot another pile of dark, mottled fur. Only this one was **moving**. It writhed and twisted, and as Melvin and Chloe looked closer, a disturbing, malformed head emerged. It was Lenny.

It *was* Lenny.

Now, this thing was no longer the golden-haired, powerful, majestic, King of the Jungle that Melvin had so often admired. His fur had turned black and had started to fall out in places, exposing numerous patches of grey, almost translucent-looking skin. His mouth hung open, allowing green saliva to drip from his blackened gums and engorged tongue. His teeth seemed to glow a toxic yellow colour, as did his drowsy, lifeless eyes. The beast was so weak it took a Herculean effort for him to lift his head from the floor. A moment later he gave in, rolling back into a ball and moaning pitifully.

"Look!" Chloe whispered, dragging Melvin's attention away from the wretched sight of Lenny's suffering and directing it back to the far wall, against which the stinking pile of monkey parts lay. This wall separated the lion enclosure from the ape house. Both were tall structures, perhaps thirty feet in height, and both had adjoining open-air sections that allowed the sunlight to come into the enclosures. From the ape house, Melvin and Chloe could see left-over parts being launched over the wall and landing on the growing pile in Lenny's cage.

"So **that's** what happened... those damn, dirty grabbles ate the monkeys, and threw the bits they didn't want over here. Lenny ate the infected parts, and they infected him," Melvin reasoned aloud.

"Wait... this could happen to **every** animal, **everywhere**! This could be the end of all life as we know it!" Chloe said. Her dramatically high-pitched voice for once perfectly suited the ever-growing seriousness of the situation. The world could be in deeper doo-doo than the zoo elephant-keeper at mucking out time.

"Well, good job we've got a solution. Let's get goi..."

Melvin was stopped in his tracks by a familiar-sounding, yet strangely altered voice...

MEEELLLᴠVIIIInNNn...

The pair spun round to see Scotty Parkinson, Melvin's best friend, at the front of a group of twenty grabbles who had snuck up behind them while they were distracted by Lenny. But it wasn't the Scotty they knew, or recognised. He seemed to have swapped his Green Oaks Primary school uniform - which now hung from his sparse frame in tatters

- for regulation 'Grabble garb'. He had the same, pallid skin as the grabbles behind him. His eyes glowed with the same, toxic, yellow luminosity and the skin on his rotting face made it look like his blackened, demonic, goo-dripping smile ran all the way from ear-to-ear. The situation had barely sunk in before Melvin and Chloe were seized by the monsters, who moved remarkably quickly for the undead, and who, more crucially, were now remarkably unbothered by leather. Melvin and Chloe's last line of defence was gone. They were dragged, kicking and screaming, towards the ape house. The zombies began to chant, and amidst the cacophony of terror, Melvin made out one word...

WWOoooODDSss... WwWoooDDssS... WWoooDDSSs... WwoooOODDSss...

Chapter 18: One of them

The ape house was a living, breathing, nightmare of a place: it swelled with the toxic sweat and painful moans of more than a hundred putrid grabbles. All the lights inside had been smashed. A sliver of daylight, which ventured through the gap in the roof at the far end of the enclosure, was all the light there was. A shifting sea of glowing, yellow, lifeless eyes stalked Melvin and Chloe through the dank space as they were hauled to the centre of the compound, stripped of their leather jackets and boots, and tossed at the foot of a piled-up mound of rocks and debris.

Scotty Parkinson, or at least, what was left of Scotty Parkinson, lumbered out from the mob which had completely surrounded the pair. He leered over Melvin, reached down with a scaly hand and pulled the black, grabble-goo-covered hockey mask off. Melvin watched in horror as Scotty's sagging face inched closer and closer, his demented smile ever-widening, his acrid breath smothering Melvin, his decaying mouth opening, his blackened, oozing teeth nearing Melvin's exposed neck...

MINEEEE...

A sudden and terrifyingly thunderous voice made Scotty recoil and retreat back into the wall of grabbles. The temporary relief Melvin felt quickly subsided when he realised that the menacing voice belonged to Mr Woods, who had appeared suddenly behind Melvin and Chloe.

He looked even more horrifying than the last time Melvin had seen him. Unlike the other grabbles, his eyes had turned from that awful milky yellow colour to the darkest black. His skin, where it still hung from his skeleton, was purple, with pulsing green veins visible underneath. His mouth hung open so wide that his bottom jaw flopped against his chest, and a bluish goo dripped from jagged, brown teeth, which appeared to have doubled in size.

There seemed to be nothing human left of Mr Woods at all.

"Mr Woods? It's me, Melvin McGee! Do you remember? From school? I was the one who threw up in your hat on that school trip to Morecambe? My mum is the one who bakes those cakes you always like at the school fair? My little sister 'freed' the class gerbil last parents' evening? Please remember!"

But it was no use, there wasn't even a hint of recognition. Mr Woods moved forward, and all the other grabbles cowered and bowed their heads as their leader approached, his twisted limbs moving awkwardly over the rocky surface. Reaching down with a skeletal hand covered in flaking flesh, Mr Woods grabbed Melvin by the neck and raised him up, so that their faces met. Melvin held on to Mr Woods' arm with one hand, and reached over his shoulder with the other...

"Oi! Woodsy!"

A shrill voice pierced the air. Mr Woods turned his head so suddenly to discover the source, that his ear flew off. It was, of course, Chloe Barnes, off on one.

"Yeah I'm talking to you, you filthy maggot-ridden rotter! You want to pick on someone? Well come down here, if you think you're hard enough! I'll kick whatever teeth you have left down your mangy throat! I'll tear your eyes out and juggle with them! I'll play your ribcage like a flipping xylophone! Come on!"

Melvin felt Mr Woods' grip loosen around his throat. He slumped to the floor, holding his neck in pain, as the grabble leader stormed (in his horribly contorted way) over to Chloe.

"Yeah that's right, let's have it! I'll slap you silly, you grotty old grabble!" Chloe continued as she lashed out aggressively, kicking and punching and clawing. But nothing she did affected Mr Woods, who reached through the cascade of blows, lifted her up by the neck and pushed the goo-covered devil mask off her face. Melvin saw, for only the second time ever, that behind all the bravery and boldness, Chloe was crying. As Mr Woods' foul mouth, filled with infectious saliva, neared her neck, Chloe turned and looked at Melvin. A last tear tumbled down her cheek as she managed to utter,

"I tried, Melvin..."

...and with that, Mr Woods sunk his poisonous teeth into Chloe's neck.

Melvin watched through a haze of burning tears as Mr Woods released Chloe and she dropped in a heap to the ground. The change started almost instantly. It was an awful sight, but Melvin couldn't bring himself to turn away, couldn't bring himself to abandon his only remaining friend. He watched as she writhed violently, twisting and screaming in agony. Patches of grey began to appear all over her, growing and joining rapidly until her healthy pink complexion had entirely disappeared beneath that same grey, translucent skin shared by the rest of the grabbles. Melvin could hear sickening cracks as her bones twisted and knotted together. Her fingers clenched and tightened into claws, and her shoulders drew up into a permanent hunch. Then came the worst part...

In the final throes of Chloe's horrific transformation, she spun around, and Melvin saw her face. He watched, tears streaming down his cheeks, as the bright blue colour drained from her eyes, only to be replaced by that awful yellow hue, seeping like spilled sour milk into her pupils. The reddish-pink colour drained from her lips, replaced by a shade of icy blue, as they might on a terribly cold day. The colour then continued to change, and soon a toxic-looking green tone set in permanently, framing a darkened mouth from which glowing, infectious saliva began to drip...

Chloe Barnes was now... one of **them**.

Mr Woods stared down at Chloe, his head lolling to one side as if he was admiring a piece of art that he had created. Then he turned his attention back to Melvin. Melvin snapped back to reality and started to scramble away, but he was fenced in by grabbles wherever he turned. They pushed and shoved him back towards their master, over and over, like cats toying with a mouse, until the final throw sent Melvin right into the hands of the King of the Grabbles. Once again, Melvin felt the zombie's rotting grasp tighten around his neck. He felt himself being lifted off the floor, then pulled in close, until he was face-to-awful-face with what remained of his old teacher. He grabbed the rotting arm again, trying as best he could to take some of the weight off his neck so that he could speak. He reached over his shoulder, feeling around, while he strained to talk...

"Mr Woods... please... it's... Melvin."

Melvin brought his hand back down and paused for a moment as he thought he saw a flash of recognition in his teacher's dark eyes. Some memory, some vague realisation of who he was...

... then the King of the Grabbles bit into Melvin's neck.

Chapter 19: The Change

The Zombie King didn't drop Melvin right away, like he had Chloe. He held him up, and he watched.

He watched the colour drain from Melvin's face, his skin turning as grey as dirty dishwater. He watched Melvin's eyes turn that same, putrid yellow. He watched Melvin writhe… and squirm… and scream.

When it was finally over, and Melvin's body had fallen still, Mr Woods lowered him slowly to the ground. However, as Mr Woods stood up, Melvin's hand remained stuck up in the air, as if it was attached to his old teacher's side. The King of the Grabbles looked down to see Melvin's grey, translucent fingers wrapped tightly around the steel shaft of a long, silver crossbow bolt, with sticky tape wrapped around one end. The other end was buried deep between Mr Woods' ribs, and unbeknownst to him, the contents of the vial were now pumping through his grabble-infected body.

Mr Woods yanked the bolt from his side and staggered back onto the mound of rocks, shaking, coughing and spluttering. The other grabbles crowded round to see, but none dared to get too close. They looked on in confusion as their leader rolled around on the floor, clutching his chest and his head. They watched as the grey, patchy skin that covered his body seemed to knit together, growing back over his skeletal frame and slowly regaining its pinky colour and fleshy plumpness. They gazed as the inky blackness withdrew from his sunken eyes, leaving them a clear, vibrant blue. They stared in shock as missing ears, a rotted nose, teeth which had dropped out and broken fingers all sprouted anew and grew back. They stood, frozen, as they witnessed the King of the Grabbles transform into a very ordinary, if very confused, Year 6 teacher from Green Oaks Primary School.

Then, one-by-one, the grabbles in the ape house collapsed to the floor, writhing violently just as Mr Woods had. Their twisted bones cricked and cracked loudly as their misshapen limbs straightened out and their contorted spines regained their normal shape. Gradually, their pallid, translucent flesh disappeared, overtaken by ever-expanding patches of smooth, healthy-looking skin which soon covered their entire bodies. Amazingly, no matter what each individual grabble was missing, all their lost parts started to grow back. For some this was a simple matter of a new ear, or a set of replacement toes. For other, more unfortunate (and less complete) grabbles, this meant whole new legs and arms. It was a remarkable sight to behold, these once rotting creatures sprouting whole new limbs and freshly made digits.

One by one, bit by bit, part by part, all the grabbles finally became what they once were...

Human.

Sadly, Scotty Parkinson still had a bit of a squint, and "Ginger" McCabe still had freckles, but hey, you can't expect miracles.

The cure was working, just like Dr Larnt said it would. It was spreading through the air from the first carrier; a powerful new anti-virus made to fight the terrible old one.

It was working... thanks to Melvin and Chloe.

Melvin still lay on the floor, clutching his head and rolling about in a limp, exhausted heap. That was, until...

"SMeLLViN! We did it!"

Melvin felt himself being dragged up off the floor. A pair of gangly arms wrapped around him, and a mess of scruffy hair mushed against his face. Chloe, as human and herself as ever, hugged him tightly.

"We did it Melvin! Look! Everyone is turning back to normal – everyone is OK!"

"We did it, Chloe... thank you."

"Ahhh, it was nothing! Now, let's get out of here... it totally smells of poo."

Chloe was right. The sickening smell of the grabbles had been replaced by the good old zoo smell of animal poop, and Melvin couldn't have been happier. Gingerly, the pair helped each other to stand up, and with an arm round each other's shoulders, they headed towards the fire exit, just outside the far end of the enclosure. Stepping over the grabble-turned humans as they went, they smiled as they watched the people they had saved all sitting up, one-by-one, rubbing their heads and looking **extremely** confused. Melvin saw one of the ex-grabbles crawling towards the main entrance, and he realised they weren't done saving the day just yet.

Melvin adopted an air-steward pose in front of the

disoriented crowd. "Emergency exits are located at the front, middle and rear of the zoo," he announced, flicking his fingers and wrists in a remarkable impersonation of experienced flight crew. "Just count the number of bones to the nearest exit to you. Don't take your hand luggage with you, and we do hope you have a safe onward journey. Thank you for flying ZombiJet Airlines," Melvin added, ushering all the bemused people through the emergency doors and out onto the street. "This way! I know you are all very confused right now, but just go home and see your families - they'll be able to explain everything, and they'll be very happy to see you, I'm sure!"

The last person to leave was Mr Woods, and as he approached he looked at Melvin and Chloe in utter disbelief and total bewilderment.

"What the...? Melvin McGee? Chloe Barnes? What are you doing here? Why aren't you at school? Why aren't I at school? What is going on? ...and what happened to my **clothes**? And... why aren't you in **UNIFORM**?"

"It's a very, very long story Mr Woods," Melvin said, his half-smile very much back in action. "Tell you what, I'll save it for show and tell. For now, you'd best just head home."

"Err... right. OK then. Erm... see you Monday?" The teacher replied as he staggered through the door.

"Of course, Sir!" Melvin replied, as he and Chloe followed their teacher out onto the street and pulled the door to behind them. "Oh, and Mr Woods?"

"Yes, Melvin?"

"Lay off the chicken for a while."

Mr Woods nodded slowly. "Will do, Melvin ... bye, then."

Chloe and Melvin looked at each other and shared a knowing smile, then set off on the long walk back to the SuperSave.

Chapter 20: Going Home

Although the now-familiar scene of devastation and carnage greeted Melvin and Chloe as they walked through the streets of Flinchester, everything seemed so much brighter. All around them, doors began to unlatch, and the previously terrified (and by this point, probably extremely hungry) occupants of Flinchester poked their heads outside for the first time in four days. Melvin and Chloe watched as confused ex-grabbles approached their respective houses, dishevelled and disorderly, only to break into the most amazing smiles and cries of joy as their loved ones came bounding out to meet them. Although they staggered along, bruised and battered, Melvin and Chloe no longer felt any of their aches or pains. Their chests were bursting with happiness at the sight of these people finding each other. **They** did that. Chloe Barnes and Melvin McGee were the saviours of Flinchester... perhaps even... the world?

"Reckon we'll get medals for this Smellvin? There's got to be some sort of prize, like a lifetime's supply of chocolate or something..."

"How about a lifetime's supply of *Flobby Jenkins Chocotastic Spread*? That would just about make this whole thing worth it!" replied Melvin, hobbling along, using his baseball bat as a walking stick.

"Well, I definitely reckon there's a shoe polish advertising contract to be had – could be worth millions."

"Ha – I'm just glad there was plenty of it in the SuperSave – it did come in handy. We wouldn't be anywhere without Doctor Larnt though. We should find him and make sure he's OK."

"I'm sure he's fine – his cure worked!"

"I wonder if it worked on grabbles like the swimming pool zombies; they were in bits last time I looked. Literally."

"Don't you remember what the doctor said? **Every** grabble, no matter how rotten they were, no matter how many bits they were missing, is now A-OK! But yeah, we'll find Doctor Larnt later. We'll even get him, like, a box of chocolates, or a tie, or a nice new pair of socks, or maybe even..."

Chloe suddenly fell silent. Ahead of them, in the middle of the road, stood a tall woman. She had frizzy blonde hair, freckles, and was frantically calling out a little girl's name.

"M-Mu-Mum?" Chloe managed, stepping forward. "... MUM!"

Chloe broke into a sprint. The woman in the road turned towards her and immediately began to run. Melvin watched as the two met and Chloe was lifted into the air. She buried her face into the woman's neck as the lady sobbed and squeezed Chloe tight. After a long, lingering hug, Chloe turned, still in the woman's arms, and pointed to Melvin. The woman began to walk towards him, still carrying Chloe, the pair speaking between hugs and smiles. As she reached Melvin, she set Chloe down, knelt down in front of Melvin, and hugged him too. Melvin was slightly taken aback, but what else should he expect from the Barnes family? Two dead arms?

"**Thank you** Melvin. Thank you **so** much. Chloe just told me that you rescued her, kept her safe from those awful **things**. Thank you. Thank you, thank you, thank you!"

"That's, err... quite alright Mrs Barnes! Chloe has looked after me too – she's been a great help and an amazing friend. I'm sure she'll tell you all about what happened!"

"We must get you home Melvin, I'll walk you back, where do you live?" Mrs Barnes asked, releasing her grip on Melvin long enough to look him in the face.

"You know what, Mrs Barnes? I think I'll be OK by myself. You get Chloe home... and don't give her any more sweets!"

"What's that supposed to mean, Smellvin?" Chloe blurted, swinging her fist and landing a perfect dead arm.

"Owww! I was only kidding!" Melvin protested, rubbing his latest wound.

"Hehe, I know!" Chloe laughed, and leaning in, she kissed him on the cheek. "Catch you later, Melvin!"

Then off Chloe went, smiling and waving as she looked backed at a slightly flushed, but very happy Melvin. He waited until they had disappeared round the corner, then he continued down the road, heading in the direction of the SuperSave.

The same burned-out cars still lay in the streets, the same felled trees still blocked the roads, the same rotting rubbish still festered on the pavements, but none of this could bring Melvin down one bit. He had done what he set out to do, he had made his family safe. He continued to half-grin as he watched more front doors slowly open, more survivors stepping out into the sunlight, more loved ones reuniting at last. As he strode on, Melvin found himself remembering what Chole had said... "Every grabble, no matter how rotten they were, no matter how many bits they were missing...." and he broke into a trot, then a gallop.

As he rounded the final corner, Melvin peered ahead towards the SuperSave. The shutters were up. Was that a good thing? Had the grabbles found their way in? Were his mum and sister OK? Melvin summoned the last tiny bit of energy he had and began to run. Yet, no sooner had he reached the pinned-up ice cream truck, did he hear a very familiar and wonderfully welcoming voice,

"MeLbbeeeN!!"

It was Jessica. She emerged from behind the old McGee family car, as scruffy and smiley as ever, followed quickly by Melvin's mum, Jane. Melvin sped forward, scooping Jessica up into his arms and carrying her on to Jane. Jane ran to meet him and wrapped her arms around her children. She sobbed tears of utter relief and absolute joy. Melvin did the same. Jessica just pulled Melvin's hair and blew snot bubbles, but he knew what she meant. He closed his eyes and buried his face into his mother's neck; she held him so tightly he thought she might never let go... and that was just fine by him...

He was home.

A moment later, Melvin felt a hand on the back of his neck. It was too big to be Jessica's, and too rough to be his mum's. He looked up from his mother's embrace...

"...Dad?"

Martin McGee was stood there, his clothes in tatters from an obviously gruelling grabble experience, but his face beaming with love and pride for his son. He took Melvin in his strong arms and lifted him high into the air, before squeezing him just as tight as he could. Melvin wrapped his arms around his dad's neck, and smiled the biggest and widest smile he'd ever smiled in his whole ten years. It even managed to spread to the other side of his face.

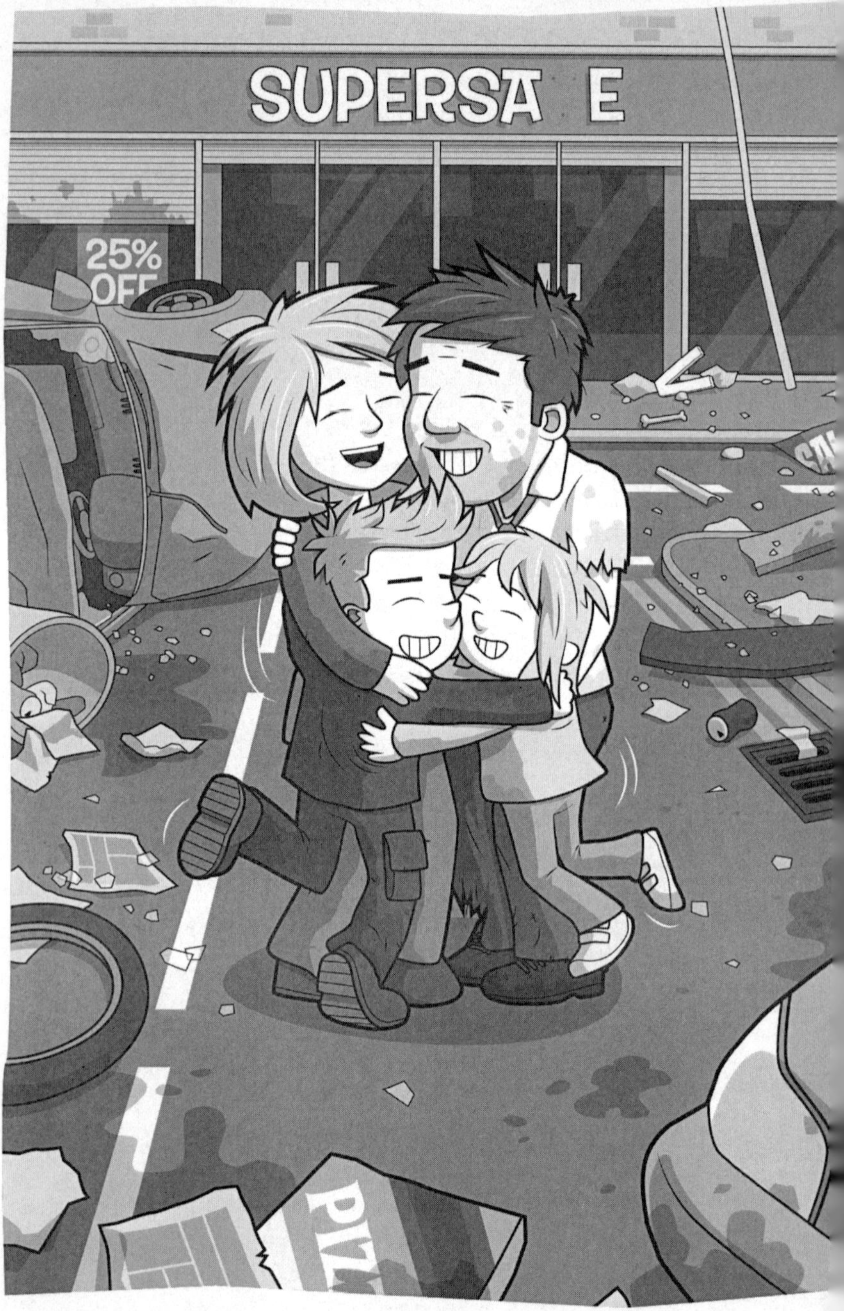
SUPERSA E
25% OFF

Chapter 21: Just Being Plain Old Melvin McGee

Two days later, the McGee family were sat round the dinner table, tucking into some proper spaghetti Bolognese, made on a proper cooker, and watching TV. They had only finished a press conference an hour before: the national news companies were hungry to know the story of the ten-year-old Zombie Hunter from Flinchester. Between that and filling in all the details of the adventure with his family, and meeting up with Doctor Larnt again, and a couple of visits to his new girlfriend's house to see how she and Gladys Stickton were getting on, it had been a crazy couple of days...

...just not quite as crazy as the previous four days.

Beaming out from the TV screen was the posh young reporter, looking much more composed (and much less sweaty) than he did the last time Melvin saw him. Without stuttering once, he managed to deliver the following report:

ACTION NEWS - CHANNEL 10

"Here is your evening news, I'm Toby Jameson. People all over the country are in the debt of a heroic ten-year-old boy today after it emerged that he was responsible for delivering the cure that stopped the spread of the recent zombie epidemic. Professor Larnt, also known as Trevor Plant, the caretaker at Green Oaks Primary School in Flinchester, appears to have been the mastermind behind the miracle antidote. We have also been informed that Melvin's friend, Chloe Barnes, and a third party, known only as 'Gladys', were indispensable in the delivery of the cure during the battle with the zombie horde. Cases of infection are now down to zero in all previously affected counties, and a full investigation into the cause of the disease, thought to be linked to genetically-modified food consumption, is already under way. For now, though, the people of Britain can sleep soundly, thanks, in no small part, to Melvin McGee: Zombie Hunter."

"So... Melvin McGee: Zombie Hunter – that's what they're calling you! Pretty impressive, son!" said Martin, looking over his newspaper at his son, who still hadn't stopped smiling.

"Ah, but there are no zombies left to hunt... whatever will you do now my little hero?" asked Jane, who also hadn't stopped smiling, and had developed a habit of hugging Melvin at least once every ten minutes.

"You know something, mum?" Melvin said, his ever-widening smile beaming brightly, "It's taken this long just to wash the smell of shoe polish out of my hair. We've got to help sort the school out, and don't get me started on the state the town is still in!

For now, I reckon I'm happy just being plain old Melvin McGee."

THE END!